D1563968

DRACULA

THE VAMPIRE PLAY IN THREE ACTS

Dramatized by

HAMILTON DEANE

AND

JOHN L. BALDERSTON

From Bram Stoker's World Famous Novel,
"Dracula"

SAMUEL FRENCH, INC.

45 WEST 25TH STREET   NEW YORK 10010

7623 SUNSET BOULEVARD HOLLYWOOD 90046

LONDON   TORONTO

Copy of original program of "DRACULA" as presented at the Fulton Theatre, New York City:

HORACE LIVERIGHT

Presents

"DRACULA"
The Vampire Play

Dramatized by Hamilton Deane and John L. Balderston
From Bram Stoker's World Famous Novel, "Dracula"

Staged by Ira Hards
General Manager and Technical Director, Louis **Cline**

CAST
(In the order of their appearance)

MISS WELLS, *maid* .... *Nedda Harrigan*
JONATHAN HARKER .... *Terence Neill*
DR. SEWARD .... *Herbert Bunston*
ABRAHAM VAN HELSING .... *Edward Van Sloan*
R. M. RENFIELD.................... *Bernard Jukes*
BUTTERWORTH .... *Albert Frith*
LUCY SEWARD .... *Dorothy Peterson*
COUNT DRACULA .... *Bela Lugosi*

ACT I. *Library in* DR. SEWARD'S *Sanatorium, Purley, England. Evening.*

ACT II. LUCY'S *Boudoir. Evening of the following day.*

ACT III. SCENE I. *The same as Act I. Thirty-two hours later. (Shortly before sunrise.)*
SCENE II. *A vault. Just after sunrise.*

Sound Effects Tape available.
$21.00, plus postage

DESCRIPTION OF CHARACTERS

DRACULA: *A tall, mysterious man. Polished and distinguished. Continental in appearance and manner. Aged fifty.*

MAID: *An attractive young girl.*

HARKER: *A young man of about twenty-five; handsome in appearance, a typical Englishman of the Public School class, but in manner direct, explosive, incisive and excitable.*

DR. SEWARD: *An alienist of about fifty-five; intelligent, but a typical specialist who lives in a world of text books and patients, not a man of action or force of character.*

ABRAHAM VAN HELSING: *A man of medium height, in the early fifties, with clean-shaven, astute face, shaggy grey eyebrows and a mass of grey hair which is brushed backward showing a high forehead. Dark, piercing eyes set far apart; nervous, alert manner; an air of resolution; clearly a man of resourceful action. Incisive speech, always to the point; raps his words out sharply and quickly.*

RENFIELD: *Repulsive youth; face distorted, shifty eyes, tousled hair.*

ATTENDANT: *Dressed in uniform.*

LUCY: *A beautiful girl of twenty, clad in filmy white dressing gown, her face unnaturally pale. She walks with difficulty; round her throat is wound a scarf.*

DRACULA

ACT ONE

SCENE: *The library on the ground floor of* DR.
SEWARD'S *Sanatorium at Purley. Room is
medieval, the walls are stone with vaulted ceiling supported by two stone pillars, but is com-
fortably furnished in modern style. Wooden
panelling around walls. Tapestries hang on the
wall. Medieval fireplace in wall* R. *Fire burning. There is a couch* R.C., *a large armchair* R.
*Flat top desk with armchair back of it Left, a
small chair* R. *of desk. Double doors, in the rear
wall* C. *and* L. *front. Large double window
across angle of room* L. *rear, leading out into
garden. The curtains at window are drawn.
Door* L.I. *Electric LIGHTS on. Invisible sliding panel in bookcase rear wall* R.*

MAID, *an attractive young girl, enters at* C.
to L. *of door, showing in* JOHN HARKER. HAR-
KER *is a young man of about twenty-five, handsome in appearance; a typical Englishman of
the Public School class, but in manner direct, explosive, incisive and excitable.*

HARKER. *(R. of door. Agitated)* You're sure
Miss Lucy is no worse?
MAID. *(Soothingly)* Just the same, sir. *(Starts
out.)*

SEWARD. *(Enters* L. *He is an alienist of about fifty-five, intelligent, but a typical specialist who lives in a world of text books and patients, not a man of action or force of character. Crosses to* C.*)* Oh! John. *(Exit* MAID C., *closing doors.)*

HARKER. *(As* SEWARD *extends hand, crossing to* L.C.*)* Doctor Seward. What is it? Why have you sent for me?

SEWARD. My dear John. I told you in my wire there was nothing new.

HARKER. You said "no change, don't worry," but to "come at once."

SEWARD. *(Approvingly)* And you lost no time.

HARKER. I jumped in the car and burned up the road from London. Oh, Doctor, surely there must be something *more* we can do for Lucy. I'd give my life gladly if it would save her.

SEWARD. I'm sure you would, my boy. You love her with the warm blood of youth, but don't forget I love my daughter, too. She's all I have. *(HARKER turns from him.)* You must see that nothing medical science can suggest has been left undone.

HARKER. *(Crosses* R. *Bitterly)* Medical science couldn't do much for Mina. Poor Mina.

SEWARD. Yes, poor Mina. She died after these same incredible symptoms that my Lucy has developed.

HARKER. My Lucy too.

SEWARD. *Our* Lucy, then. *(Crosses to* L. *end of desk. Wild, maniacal LAUGH is heard off* L.U.*)*

HARKER. *(Moves up to* L. *of sofa)* Good God, what was that?

SEWARD. *(Sits* L. *of desk)* Only Renfield. A patient of mine.

HARKER. *(Crosses to* L.C.*)* But you never keep violent patients here in your sanatorium. Lucy mustn't be compelled to listen to raving madmen.

SEWARD. I quite agree, and I'm going to have him

sent away. Until just lately he was always quiet.
I'll be sorry to lose him.

HARKER. What!

SEWARD. An unusual case. Zoophagous.

HARKER. What's that?

SEWARD. A life-eating maniac.

HARKER. What?

SEWARD. Yes, he thinks that by absorbing lives he
can prolong his own life.

HARKER. Good Lord!

SEWARD. Catches flies and eats them. And by way
of change, he feeds flies to spiders. Fattens them
up. Then he eats the spiders.

HARKER. Good God, how disgusting. (Crosses to
chair R. of desk and sits) But tell me about Lucy.
(Leans over desk) Why did you send for me?

SEWARD. Yesterday I wired to Holland for my
old friend Van Helsing. He'll be here soon. The
car has gone down to the station for him now. I'm
going to turn Lucy's case over to him.

HARKER. Another specialist on anæmia?

SEWARD. No, my boy, whatever this may be, it's
not anæmia, and this man, who speaks a dozen lan-
guages as well as his own, knows more about mysterious diseases than anyone alive.

HARKER. (Rises; step down R.) Heaven knows
it's mysterious enough, but surely the symptoms are
clear.

SEWARD. So were poor Mina's. Perfectly clear.
(A DOG HOWLS at a distance. Other dogs take
up the lugubrious chorus far and near. SEWARD
rises; crosses to fireplace) There they are, at it
again, every dog for a mile around.

HARKER. (Crosses to window) They seem howls
of terror.

SEWARD. We've heard that chorus every night
since Mina fell ill.

HARKER. (Crosses to above desk) When I was

travelling in Russia, and the dogs in the village barked like that, the natives always said wolves were prowling about.

SEWARD. *(Gets cigarette on mantel; lights it)* I hardly think you'll find wolves prowling around Purley, twenty miles from London.

HARKER. *(Crosses to window)* Yet your old house might be in a wilderness. *(Looks out of window)* Nothing in sight except that place Carfax that Count Dracula has taken.

SEWARD. *(Turning from fireplace)* Your friend, the Count, came in again last evening.

HARKER. He's no friend of mine. *(Crosses to L. end of divan.)*

SEWARD. Don't say that. He knows that you and I gave our blood for Lucy as well as for Mina, and he's offered to undergo transfusion himself if we need another volunteer. *(Sits on divan.)*

HARKER. By Jove, that's sporting of him. I see I've misjudged him.

SEWARD. He seems genuinely interested in Lucy. If he were a young man I'd think——

HARKER. What!

SEWARD. But his whole attitude shows that it isn't that. We need sympathy in this house, John, and I'm grateful for it.

HARKER. So am I. Anyone who offers to help Lucy can have anything I've got.

SEWARD. Well, I think he does help Lucy. She always seems cheered up when he comes.

HARKER. That's fine. May I go to Lucy now?

SEWARD. *(Rises)* We'll go together. *(Crosses L. BELL rings off. HARKER crosses to door L. SEW-APL crosses down L.; puts out cigarette in ashtray)* That must be Van Helsing. You go ahead and I'll come presently. *(HARKER exits L.)*

(MAID *shows in* ABRAHAM VAN HELSING, *who en-*

ters L. *briskly. Man of medium height, in the early fifties, with clean-shaven, astute face, shaggy grey eyebrows and a mass of grey hair which is brushed backward showing a high forehead. Dark, piercing eyes set far apart; nervous, alert manner; an air of resolution, clearly a man of resourceful action. Incisive speech, always to the point; raps his words out sharply and quickly.* VAN HELSING *carries small black bag.*)

MAID. Professor Van Helsing!

SEWARD. *(Crosses* L.C. *He and* VAN HELSING *shake hands warmly as* MAID *goes out* C.) My dear Van Helsing, I can never repay you for this.

VAN HELSING. *(*R.C.*)* Were it only a patient of yours instead of your daughter, I would have come. You once rendered me a service.

SEWARD. Don't speak of that. You'd have done it for me. *(Starts to ring)* Let me give you something to eat. *(Moves one step up, stopped by* VAN HELSING'S *gesture.)*

VAN HELSING. *(Crosses; places bag on table back of sofa)* I dined on the boat train. I do not waste time when there is work to do. *(Crosses back to* C.)

SEWARD. Ah, Van Helsing, you cast the old spell on me. I lean on you before you have been two minutes in my house.

VAN HELSING. You wrote of your daughter's symptoms. Tell me more of the other young lady, the one who died.

SEWARD. *(Crosses* L.; *shows* VAN HELSING *chair* R. *of desk. He sits.* SEWARD *sits* L. *desk)* Poor Mina Weston. She was a girl just Lucy's age. They were inseparable. She was on a visit here when she fell ill. As I wrote you, she just grew weaker, day by day she wasted away. But there were no anæmic symptoms, her blood was normal when analyzed.

VAN HELSING. You said you performed transfusion.

SEWARD. Yes, Sir William Briggs ordered that. *(Baring forearm)* You see this mark? Well, Lucy herself, and her fiancee, John Harker, gave their blood as well.

VAN HELSING. So—— Three transfusions—— And the effect?

SEWARD. She rallied after each. The color returned to her cheeks, but the next morning she would be pale and weak again. She complained of *bad dreams.* Ten days ago we found her in a stupor from which nothing could rouse her. She—died.

VAN HELSING. And—the other symptoms?

SEWARD. None, except those two little marks on the throat that I wrote you about.

VAN HELSING. And which perhaps brought me here so quickly. What were they like?

SEWARD. Just two little white dots with red centers. (VAN HELSING *nods grimly.)* We decided she must have run a safety pin through the skin of her throat, trying in her delirium to fasten a scarf or shawl.

VAN HELSING. Perhaps. And your daughter's symptoms are the same?

SEWARD. Precisely. She too speaks of *bad dreams.* Van Helsing, you've lived in the tropics. May this not be something alien to our medical experience in England?

VAN HELSING. *(Grimly)* It may indeed, my friend. *(LAUGH is heard from behind curtain at window.* SEWARD *rises, after* VAN HELSING *rises, and* SEWARD *crosses to up* R. *of window and draws curtains.* RENFIELD *is standing there. Repulsive youth, face distorted, shifty eyes, tousled hair.* VAN HELSING *back to* R.C.*)*

SEWARD. *(Astounded, drawing* RENFIELD *into room)* Renfield. How did you——?

VAN HELSING. Who is this man?

SEWARD. *(Crosses to bell up* C.; *rings)* One of my patients. This is gross carelessness.

VAN HELSING. Did you hear us talking?

RENFIELD. Words—words—words——

SEWARD. Come, come, Renfield, you know you mustn't wander about this way. How did you get out of your room?

RENFIELD. *(Crosses down to* C.; *laughs)* Wouldn't you like to know?

SEWARD. *(Crosses to below desk)* How are the flies? *(To* VAN HELSING*)* Mr. Renfield makes a hobby of eating flies. I'm afraid you eat spiders, too, sometimes. Don't you, Renfield?

RENFIELD. Will you walk into my parlor, said the spider to the fly. Excuse me, Doctor, you have not introduced me to your friend.

SEWARD. *(Reprovingly)* Come, come, Renfield.

VAN HELSING. Humor him. *(Enter* MAID C.*)*

SEWARD. Tell the Attendant to come here at once.

MAID. Yes, sir. *(Exit* C.*)*

SEWARD. Oh, very well. Professor Van Helsing, Mr. Renfield, a patient of mine. (VAN HELSING *steps toward him.* SEWARD L. *of desk. They shake hands.* VAN HELSING *rubs* RENFIELD'S *fingers with his thumb and* RENFIELD *jerks hand away.)*

RENFIELD. Ah, who does not know of Van Helsing. Your work, sir, in investigating certain obscure diseases, not altogether unconnected with forces and powers that the ignorant herd do not believe exist, has won you a position that posterity will recognize. *(Enter* ATTENDANT C., *dressed in uniform. He starts at seeing* RENFIELD, *then looks at* SEWARD *sheepishly.)*

SEWARD. *(A step* R. *of desk. As severely as his mild nature permits)* Butterworth, you have let your patient leave his room again.

ATTENDANT. Blimme, sir, I locked the door on 'im, and I've got the key in my pocket now.

SEWARD. But this is the second time. Only last night you let him escape and he tried to break into Count Dracula's house across the grounds.

ATTENDANT. *(Crossing down)* 'E didn't get out the door this time, sir, and it's a drop of thirty feet out of the windows. *(Points to window. Crosses to* RENFIELD*)* He's just a bloomin' eel. Now you come with me. *(As they start toward door* C.; *holds* RENFIELD *by coat collar and right arm.)*

SEWARD. Renfield, if this happens again you will get no more sugar to spread out for your flies.

RENFIELD. *(Drawing himself up)* What do I care for flies—*now?* (ATTENDANT *gives* VAN HELSING *a look.)* Flies. Flies are but poor things. *(As he speaks he follows with his eyes a fly.* ATTENDANT *sees fly too; releases* RENFIELD *indulgently. With a sweep of his hand he catches fly, holds closed hand to ear as if listening to buzz of fly as he crosses a few steps* L., *then carries it to his mouth. Then seeing them watching him, releases it quickly)* A low form of life. Beneath my notice. I don't care a pin about flies.

ATTENDANT. Oh, doncher? Any more o' yer tricks and I'll take yer new spider away.

RENFIELD. *(Babbles—on knees)* Oh, no, no! Please, dear Mr. Butterworth, please leave me my spider. He's getting so nice and fat. When he's had another dozen flies he'll be just right, just right. *(Gives little laugh. Rubs hands together, then catches fly and makes gesture of eating.)*

VAN HELSING. Come, Mr. Renfield, what makes you want to eat flies?

RENFIELD. *(Rises.* ATTENDANT *backs up a few steps)* The wings of a fly, my dear sir, typify the aerial powers of the psychic faculties.

SEWARD. *(To* ATTENDANT, *wearily)* Butterworth, take him away.

VAN HELSING. One moment, my friend. *(To* RENFIELD*)* And the spiders?

RENFIELD. *(Crosses to* VAN HELSING. *Impressively)* Professor Van Helsing, can you tell me why that one great spider lived for centuries in the tower of the old Spanish church—and grew and grew? He never ate, but he drank, and he *drank.* He would come down and drink the oil of all the church lamps.

SEWARD. *(To* ATTENDANT*)* Butterworth. (AT-TENDANT *takes step down.)*

RENFIELD. *(Crosses to* SEWARD*)* One moment, Doctor Seward—— (VAN HELSING *gets wolf's-bane from bag on table above sofa and moves back to* R.C.*)* I want you to send me away, now, *tonight,* in a straight waistcoat. Chain me so I can't escape. This is a sanatorium, not a lunatic asylum. This is no place for me. My cries will disturb Miss Lucy, who is ill. They will give your daughter *bad dreams,* Doctor Seward, *bad dreams.*

SEWARD. *(Soothingly)* We'll see about all this in the morning. *(Nods to* ATTENDANT, *who takes half step toward* RENFIELD.*)*

VAN HELSING. Why are you so anxious to go?

RENFIELD. *(Crosses to* VAN HELSING; *hesitates with gesture of decision)* I'll tell *you.* Not that fool Seward. He wouldn't understand. But you— *(A large BAT dashes against window.* RENFIELD *turns to the window, holds out his hands and gibbers. Crosses to window)* No, no, no, I wasn't going to say anything—— (ATTENDANT *crosses up; watches* RENFIELD.*)*

SEWARD. *(Moves step up* L.*)* What was that?

RENFIELD. *(Looks out window, then turns; moves toward* C.*)* It was a bat, gentleman. Only a bat. Do you know that in some islands of the East-

ern seas there are bats which hang on trees all night?
And when the heat is stifling and sailors sleep on
the deck in those harbors, in the morning *they* are
found dead men—white, even as Miss Mina was.

SEWARD. What do you know of Miss Mina?
(Pause.) Take him to his room. (ATTENDANT *half
step down.)*

VAN HELSING. *(To* SEWARD*)* Please! *(To* REN-
FIELD*)* Why are you so anxious to be moved from
here?

RENFIELD. To save my soul.

VAN HELSING. Yes?

RENFIELD. Oh, you'll get nothing more out of me
than that. And I'm not sure I hadn't rather stay—
After all, what is my soul good for? Is not—*(Turns
to window) —what I am to receive worth* the loss
of my soul?

SEWARD. *(Lightly)* What's got him thinking about
souls? Have you the souls of those flies and spiders
on your conscience?

RENFIELD. *(During* SEWARD'S *speech puts fingers
in his ears, shuts eyes, distorts face, crosses* L.*)* I
forbid you to plague me about souls. I don't want
their souls. All I want is their life. The blood is
the life——

VAN HELSING. So?

RENFIELD. That's in the Bible. What use are
souls to me? *(Crosses to* VAN HELSING*)* I couldn't
eat them or dr—— *(Breaks off suddenly.)*

VAN HELSING. Or drink—— *(Holding wolf's-
bane under his nose,* RENFIELD'S *face becomes convulsed with rage and loathing. He leaps back.)*

RENFIELD. You know too much to live, Van Helsing. *(Attacking* VAN HELSING. ATTENDANT *at* R.
of RENFIELD; *shout from him and* SEWARD *at attack. As* ATTENDANT *and* SEWARD *drag* RENFIELD,
*struggling, to door he stops struggling and says
clearly)* I'll go quietly. *(SEWARD lets go of him*

crosses to above desk. To SEWARD*)* I warned you to send me away. Doctor Seward, if you don't you must answer for my soul before the judgment seat of God. *(Exit* ATTENDANT *and* RENFIELD, C. *WILD LAUGH during exit can be heard off.* VAN HEL-SING *puts wolf's-bane in bag and crosses down* L. SEWARD *closes door.* VAN HELSING *walks* R.C.*)*

SEWARD. My friend, you're not hurt?

VAN HELSING. No.

SEWARD. *(Crosses down* R.C.*)* My deepest apologies. You'll think my place shockingly managed— *(Crosses to* L. *of sofa.* VAN HELSING *crosses down* L. *of desk and to window.* VAN HELSING *waves apology aside with impatient gesture.)* What was your herb that excited him so?

VAN HELSING. Wolf's-bane. *(Crosses to up* L.C.; *little look out of window as he passes.)*

SEWARD. Wolf's-bane? What's that? I thought I knew all the drugs in the pharmacopoeia.

VAN HELSING. *(Crosses to* L.C.*)* One of the— eremophytes. Pliny the Elder mentions the plant. It grows only in the wilds of Central Russia.

SEWARD. But why did you bring it with you?

VAN HELSING. It is a form of preventive medicine. *(Steps up.)*

SEWARD. Well, we live and learn. I never heard of it.

VAN HELSING. Seward, I want you to have that lunatic securely watched.

SEWARD. *(Move* L. *toward him)* Anything you say, Doctor Van Helsing, but it's my Lucy I want you to look after first.

VAN HELSING. I want to keep this man under observation.

SEWARD. *(Annoyed and hurt)* An interesting maniac, no doubt, but surely you'll see my daughter.

VAN HELSING. I must see the records of his case.

SEWARD. But Doctor——

Van Helsing. Do you think I have forgotten why I am here?

Seward. *(As they go out* L. Seward *crosses first, opening door for* Van Helsing*)* Forgive me. Of course I'll show you the records, but I don't understand why you're so curious about Renfield, because in your vast experience—— *(Exit* L. *Stage empty for a few seconds.)*

(Enter Lucy c., *supported by* Harker *on her* R. *She is a beautiful girl of twenty, clad in filmy white dressing gown, her face unnaturally pale. She walks with difficulty. Round her throat is wound a scarf. She crosses to* R. *of desk and leans on it as* Harker *closes door.)*

Harker. *(Crosses to her and supports her)* Why, I thought they were here, Lucy.

Lucy. John, do you think this new man will be any better than the others?

Harker. *(Moving her to sofa)* I'm sure he will. Anyway, Lucy, now that I'm back I'm going to stay with you till you get over this thing.

Lucy. *(Delighted)* Oh, John. But can you? Your work in town?

Harker. *(Seating her* L. *end of sofa, he sits* R. *of her)* You come first.

Lucy. *(A change comes over her)* I—don't think you'd better stay, John. *(A look about room)* Sometimes—I feel that I want to be alone. *(Facing away from him.)*

Harker. *(Hurt)* My dear. How can you say that you don't want me with you when you're so ill? You love me, don't you? *(Taking her hand.)*

Lucy. *(Affectionately)* Yes, John, with all my soul.

Harker. Just as soon as you're well enough I'm going to take you away. We'll be married next

month. We won't wait till June. We'll stretch that
honeymoon month to three months and the house
will be ready in July.

LUCY. *(Overjoyed)* John, you think we could?

HARKER. Of course, why not? My mother wanted
us to wait, but she'll understand, and I want to get
you *away——* *(Starts to kiss her. She shudders as
he does so.)* Why do you shrink when I kiss you?
You're so cold, Lucy, always so cold—now——

LUCY. *(With tenderness but no hint of passion)*
Forgive me, dear. I am yours, all yours. *(Clings
to him. He embraces her. She sinks back)* Oh,
John, I'm so tired—so tired. (SEWARD *enters* L.
VAN HELSING *enters; crosses to* L. *of sofa.* SEW-
ARD *closes door; crosses to* C. HARKER *rises; moves*
R.*)*

SEWARD. Lucy dear, this is my old friend, Professor Van Helsing. *(She sits up; extends her hand
to him.)*

VAN HELSING. *(Below sofa,* L. *of her)* My dear
Miss Seward—(VAN HELSING *kisses* LUCY's *hand)*
—you don't remember poor old Van Helsing. I
knew you when you were a little girl. So high—and
now what charm, what beauty. A little pale, yes, but
we will bring the roses back to the cheeks.

LUCY. You were so kind to come, Professor.

VAN HELSING. And this, no doubt, is the fortu-
nate young man you are to marry?

SEWARD. Yes, John Harker, Professor. *(They
bow to each other.)*

HARKER. *(Down extreme* R.*)* Look here, Professor. I'm not going to get in your way, but if
Doctor Seward will have me I'm going to make him
give me a bed here until Lucy gets over this thing.
(Turns to SEWARD*)* It's absolute hell, being away
in London, and of course I can't do any work.

SEWARD. *(Crosses to above* L. *of sofa)* You're
most welcome to stay, my boy.

VAN HELSING. Indeed, yes. I should have asked you to stay. I may need you. *(Takes chair from desk to L. of divan; turns to* LUCY *on divan)* Now lie back, so—— *(Examines her eyelids carefully and feels her pulse.* SEWARD *above back of divan.)* And now tell me when did this, this weakness first come upon you? *(Sits chair L. of sofa after examining eyelids; crosses, looks at her gums, examines tips of finger nails, then takes out watch as he feels her pulse.)*

LUCY. *(Looks at* VAN HELSING, *then front)* Two nights after poor Mina was buried I had—a bad dream.

VAN HELSING. *(Releases pulse, after looking at watch)* A bad dream? Tell me about it.

LUCY. I remember hearing dogs barking before I went to sleep. The air seemed oppressive. I left the reading lamp lit by my bed, but when the dream came there seemed to come a mist in the room.

VAN HELSING. Was the window open?

LUCY. Yes, I always sleep with my window open.

VAN HELSING. Oh, of course, you're English. *(Laughs.* SEWARD *joins laugh.)* We Continentals are not so particular about fresh air. And then——

LUCY. *(Looks at him, then out front)* The mist seemed so thick I could just see the lamp by my bed, a tiny spark in the fog, and then—— *(Hysterically)* I saw two red eyes staring at me and a livid white face looking down on me out of the mist. It was horrible, horrible. *(Hands covering face.* HARKER *makes move toward her.* VAN HELSING *stops him by a gesture.)*

VAN HELSING. There, there—— *(Soothingly, taking her hands from her face)* Go on, please.

LUCY. *(Gives little start when* VAN HELSING *touches her hands. Looks at* HARKER *and starts—and at* SEWARD *and starts, then at* VAN HELSING *and relaxes)* The next morning my maid could scarcely wake me. I felt weak and languid. Some part of my life seemed to have gone from me.

VAN HELSING. There have been other such dreams?

LUCY. Nearly every night since then has come the mist—the red eyes and that awful face. *(Puts hands to her face again. VAN HELSING soothes her; ad libs. as he takes her hands from face, "There, there, now.")*

SEWARD. We've tried transfusion twice. Each time she recovered her strength.

LUCY. But then would come another dream. And now I dread the night. I know it seems absurd, Professor, but please don't laugh at me. *(Turns to him; takes his hand as he reassures her.)*

VAN HELSING. I'm not likely to laugh—— *(Gently, without answering, unwinds scarf from her throat. She puts hand up to stop him and cries, "No, no." A look at HARKER when her neck is bare. As VAN HELSING does so he starts, then quickly opens small black bag on table and returns with microscope; examines two small marks on throat. LUCY with eyes closed. Controlling himself with difficulty, VAN HELSING puts microscope back in bag, closes it, puts back chair by desk, and crosses to c.)* And how long have you had these little marks on your throat? *(SEWARD and HARKER start violently and come to couch. They look at each other in horror.)*

LUCY. Since—that first morning.

HARKER. Lucy, why didn't you tell us?

SEWARD. Lucy, you've worn that scarf around your throat—to hide them. *(LUCY makes convulsive clutch at throat.)*

VAN HELSING. Do not press her. Do not excite her. *(Crosses to L. end of divan. To LUCY)* Well?

LUCY. *(Constrained—to SEWARD and HARKER)* I

was afraid they'd worry you, for I knew that—Mina had them.

VAN HELSING. *(With assumed cheerfulness)* Quite right, Miss Lucy, quite right. They're nothing, and old Van Helsing will see that these—dreams trouble you no more. (SEWARD *moves a step up to above* R. *end of divan.)*

MAID. *(Appears in door* C.) Count Dracula. *(Step to* L. *of door* C. MAID *stands* L. *of door.* DRACULA *enters.* LUCY *registers attraction to* DRACULA.)

SEWARD. Ah, good evening, Count.

DRACULA. Gentlemen—— *(Bows to* MEN. *Walks down* C.; *bows in courtly fashion)* Miss Seward, how are you? You are looking more yourself this evening. (LUCY *registers thrill. Alternate moods of attraction and repulsion, unaccountable to hers lf, affect* LUCY *in* DRACULA'S *presence. But this should be suggested subtly.)*

LUCY. *(Quite natural)* I feel better already, Count, now that father's old friend has come to help me. (DRACULA *turns to* VAN HELSING. LUCY *looks up at* DRACULA *and recoils and turns to* HARKER.)

SEWARD. Count Dracula, Professor Van Helsing. *(The two* MEN *bow.)*

DRACULA. *(Crosses down a few steps; bows to* VAN HELSING) A most distinguished scientist, whose name we know even in the wilds of Transylvania. *(To* SEWARD) But I interrupt a consultation.

SEWARD. Not at all, Count. It's good of you to come, and we appreciate your motives.

HARKER. Doctor Seward has just told me of your offer, and I can't thank you enough.

DRACULA. It is nothing. I should be grateful to be permitted to help Miss Lucy in any way.

LUCY. But you do, Count. I look forward to your visits. They seem to make me better.

VAN HELSING. *(Crosses to* MAID *up* L.; *whispers to her)* And so I arrive to find a rival in the field.

DRACULA. *(Crosses to* LUCY*)* You encourage me, Miss Seward, to make them more frequent, as I should like to.

LUCY. *(Looking at him fixedly)* I am always glad to see you.

DRACULA. Ah, but you have been lonely here. And my efforts to amuse you with our old tales will no longer have the same success, now that you have Professor Van Helsing with you, and especially now that Mr. Harker is to remain here.

HARKER. *(Crosses* L. *few steps)* How did you know I was going to stay, Count?

DRACULA. *(Little start)* Can the gallant lover ask such a question? I inferred it, my friend.

HARKER. You're right. Nothing is going to shift me now until Lucy's as fit as a fiddle again.

DRACULA. Nothing?

LUCY. Please come as before, Count, won't you? *(*DRACULA *bows to her; kisses her hand.* VAN HELSING *meanwhile has been talking to* MAID *upstage.)*

VAN HELSING. —you understand, you will not answer bells. She must not be alone for a single moment under any circumstances, you understand. *(*DRACULA *crosses* L. *to below desk. As* DRACULA *crosses* L., LUCY *leans toward* DRACULA, *extends her hand, then recovers herself.* VAN HELSING *registers that he sees her look at* DRACULA.*)*

MAID. Yes, sir.

VAN HELSING. *(Coming down to* LUCY. MAID *comes down to get* LUCY*)* Good. Your maid will take you to your room. Try to rest for a little, while I talk to your father. *(*MAID *takes* LUCY *a few steps. Pause as* LUCY *looks at* DRACULA, *then up* C.*)*

SEWARD. Wells, remember, don't leave her alone for a moment. *(*DRACULA *circles* L. *of desk and* *down* L.C. MAID *takes* LUCY *out* C. LUCY *exchanges a long look with* DRACULA.)

MAID. Oh, no, sir. (SEWARD *crosses down* R. *to below the couch as soon as* LUCY *crosses up.)*

DRACULA. *(To* VAN HELSING, *crossing down* L.C.*)* Professor Van Helsing, so you have come from the land of the tulip, to cure the nervous prostration of this charming girl. I wish you all the success.

VAN HELSING. Thank you, Count.

DRACULA. *(Crosses to* C. SEWARD *below* L. *end of couch.* HARKER *crosses down* R. *by fireplace)* Do I appear officious, Doctor Seward? I am a lonely man. You are my only neighbors when I am here at Carfax, and your trouble has touched me greatly.

SEWARD. Count, I am more grateful for your sympathy than I can say.

VAN HELSING. You, like myself, are a stranger in England, Count?

DRACULA. Yes, but I love England and the great London—so different from my own Transylvania, where there are so few people and so little opportunity. *(Faces directly front on "so little opportunity.")*

VAN HELSING. Opportunity, Count?

DRACULA. *(Bows)* For my investigations, Professor. (VAN HELSING *bows to him.)*

SEWARD. I hope you haven't regretted buying that old ruin across there? (HARKER *crosses to* R. *of divan.)*

DRACULA. Oh, Carfax is not a ruin. The dust was somewhat deep, but we are used to dust in Transylvania.

HARKER. *(Step* R.*)* You plan to remain in England, Count?

DRACULA. I think so, my friend. The walls of my castle are broken, and the shadows are many, and I am the last of my race.

HARKER. It's a lonely spot you've chosen—Carfax.

DRACULA. It is, and when I hear the dogs howling far and near I think myself back in my castle Dracula with its broken battlements.

HARKER. Ah, the dogs howl there when there are wolves around, don't they?

DRACULA. They do, my friend. And they howl here as well, although there are no wolves. But you wish to consult the anxious father and the great specialist. *(Bows to* VAN HELSING. SEWARD *crosses around* R. *end of divan, glances at* HARKER; *to meet* DRACULA *at* R. *of door.* DRACULA *to door* C.*)* May I read a book in the study? I am so anxious to hear what the Professor says—and to learn if I can be of any help.

SEWARD. By all means, Count. *(*DRACULA *bows; exits* C. *DOGS howl off stage.* SEWARD *watches* DRACULA *exit, then crosses below and* L. *of sofa.* VAN HELSING *crosses to window.)* Very kind of Dracula, with his damned untimely friendliness, but now what about my daughter?

HARKER. Yes, Professor, what do you think is the matter with Lucy?

VAN HELSING. *(Crosses to window, looks out, then crosses down* L.C. *Long pause before he speaks)* Your patient, that interesting Renfield, does not like the smell of wolf's-bane.

SEWARD. Good Heavens. What has that got to do with Lucy?

VAN HELSING. Perhaps nothing.

HARKER. In God's name, Professor, is there anything unnatural or occult about this business?

SEWARD. *(Holds position just in front of the* L. *end of divan)* Occult? Van Helsing! Oh——

VAN HELSING. Ah, Seward, let me remind you that the superstitions of today are the scientific facts of tomorrow. Science can now transmute the electron, the basis of all matter, into energy, and what is that but the dematerialization of matter? Yet dematerialization has been known and practised in India for centuries. In Java I myself have seen things.

SEWARD. My dear old friend, you can't have filled up your fine old brain with Eastern moonshine.

VAN HELSING. Moonshine?

SEWARD. But anyway, come now, what about my daughter?

VAN HELSING. Ah! Seward, if you won't listen to what will be harder to believe than any Eastern moonshine, if you won't forget your textbooks—keep an open mind, then, Seward. Your daughter's life may pay for your pig-headedness.

HARKER. Go on, go on, Professor!

SEWARD. I am listening.

VAN HELSING. Then I must ask you to listen calmly to what I am going to say. Sit down. (VAN HELSING *crosses to window; closes curtains.* SEWARD *and* HARKER *exchange glances, then* BOTH *look at* VAN HELSING *as they sit.* SEWARD *sits* L. *end of divan.* HARKER *in chair* R. VAN HELSING *in chair he gets from desk and places* L. *of divan.*) You have both heard the legends of Central Europe, about the Werewolf, the Vampires?

SEWARD. You mean ghosts, who suck the blood of the living?

VAN HELSING. If you wish to call them ghosts. I call them the undead.

HARKER. (*Quickly*) For God's sake, man, are you suggesting that Mina, and now Lucy——

SEWARD. (*Interrupting*) Of course, I have read these horrible folk tales of the Middle Ages, Van Helsing, but I know you better than to suppose——

VAN HELSING. (*Interrupting*) That I believe them? I *do* believe them.

SEWARD. (*Incredulously*) You mean to tell us

that vampires actually exist and—and that Mina
and Lucy have been attacked by one?

VAN HELSING. Your English doctors would all
laugh at such a theory. Your police, your public
would laugh. *(Impressively) The strength of the
vampire is that people will not believe in him.*

SEWARD. *(Shaking head, looks away from VAN
HELSING)* Is this the help you bring us?

VAN HELSING. *(Much moved)* Do not despise it.

HARKER. *(To SEWARD)* Doctor, this case has
stumped all your specialists. *(To VAN HELSING)*
Go on, Professor. (SEWARD *looks at* VAN HEL-
SING.)

VAN HELSING. Vampires are rare. Nature ab-
hors them, the forces of good combine to destroy
them, but a few of these creatures have lived on
for centuries.

HARKER. *(Excited)* What *is* a vampire?

VAN HELSING. A vampire, my friend, is a man
or a woman who is dead and yet not dead. A thing
that lives after its death by drinking the blood of
the living. It must have blood or it dies. Its power
lasts only from sunset to sunrise. During the hours
of the day it must rest in the earth in which it was
buried. But, during the night, it has the power to
prey upon the living. *(To SEWARD. Incredulous
move from SEWARD)* My friend, you are thinking
you will have to put me amongst your patients?

SEWARD. Van Helsing, I don't know what to think
but I confess I simply can't follow you.

HARKER. What makes you think that Lucy has
been attacked by such a creature?

VAN HELSING. *(From now on dominating them.
SEWARD looks at him)* Doctor Seward's written ac-
count of these ladies' symptoms at once aroused my
suspicion. Anæmia? The blood of three men was
forced into the veins of Miss Mina. Yet she died
from loss of blood. Where did it go? Had your

specialist any answer? The vampire attacks the throat. He leaves two little wounds, white with red centres. (HARKER *rises slowly.*) Seward, you wrote me of those two marks on Miss Mina's throat. An accident with a safety-pin, you said. So I thought, I suspected, I did not know, but I came on the instant, and what do I find? These same wounds on Miss Lucy's throat. Another safety-pin, Doctor Seward?

SEWARD. Do you mean to say that you've built up all this nightmare out of a safety-pin? It's true I can't make out why she hid those marks from us.

VAN HELSING. I could tell you that.

SEWARD. *(Pause)* What! I don't believe it. Of course Lucy's trouble can't be *that*.

HARKER. *(A few steps* L.*)* I do believe it. This theory accounts for all the facts that nobody has been able to explain. We'll take her away where this thing can't get at her.

VAN HELSING. She will not want to go.

SEWARD. What!

VAN HELSING. If you force her, the shock may be fatal.

HARKER. But why won't she go if we tell her that her life depends on it?

VAN HELSING. Because the victim of the vampire becomes his creature, linked to him in life and after death.

SEWARD. *(Horrified, incredulous, shocked; rises; crosses* L. *to below end of desk)* Professor, this is too much!

HARKER. Lucy become an unclean thing, a demon? (SEWARD *stops on the word "demon"; turns* R.*)*

VAN HELSING. *(To* HARKER; *rises)* Yes, Harker. *Now* will you help me?

HARKER. Yes, anything. Tell me what to do.

VAN HELSING. It is dangerous work. Our lives are at stake, but so is Miss Lucy's life, so is her soul.

We must stamp out this monster. *(Turns* L. *to* SEW-ARD.)

HARKER. How can we stamp it out now?

VAN HELSING. This undead thing lies helpless **by** day in the earth or tomb in which it was buried.

SEWARD. A corpse, in a coffin? *(A step* R.)

VAN HELSING. A corpse, if you like, but a living corpse, sustained by the blood of the living. If we can find its earth home, a stake driven through the heart destroys the vampire. But this is our task. In such a case the police, all the powers of society, are as helpless as the doctors. What bars or chains can hold a creature who can turn into a wolf or a bat?

HARKER. A wolf! Doctor Seward, those dogs howling! I told you they howl that way in Russia when wolves are about. And a bat—Renfield said there was a bat.

SEWARD. *(Another step in to* L.C.) Well. What of it?

VAN HELSING. *(Reflectively)* Your friend Renfield does not like the smell of wolf's-bane.

SEWARD. But what in the world has your wolf's-bane to do with all this?

VAN HELSING. A vampire cannot stand the smell of wolf's-bane.

HARKER. You suspect that lunatic?

VAN HELSING. I suspect no one and everyone. *(Crosses to* SEWARD) Tell me, who is this Count Dracula?

SEWARD. *(Crosses up a few steps)* Dracula? We really know very little about him.

HARKER. When I was in Transylvania I heard of Castle Dracula. A famous Voivode Dracula who fought the Turks lived there centuries ago.

VAN HELSING. I will make inquiries by telegraph. No, but after all this thing must be English. *(Crosses* L.) Or at least have died here. His lair must be

near enough to this house for him to get back there
before sunrise. *(Turns back* L.C. *To* SEWARD*)* Oh,
my friend, I have only the old beliefs with which
to fight this monster that has the strength of twenty
men, perhaps the accumulated wisdom and cunning
of centuries.

HARKER. This all seems a nightmare. But I'm
with you, Professor.

VAN HELSING. And you, Doctor Seward?

SEWARD. It all seems preposterous to me. But
everyone else has failed. The case is in your hands
at present *(Moves up.)*

VAN HELSING. *(Sternly)* I need allies, not neu-
trals.

SEWARD. *(Turns down)* Very well, then, do what
you will.

VAN HELSING. Good. Then bring your daughter
here.

SEWARD. What are you going to do?

VAN HELSING. To set a trap. Miss Lucy is the
bait.

HARKER. My God, we can't let you do that.
(Crosses a few steps C.*)*

VAN HELSING. *(Crosses to* R.C.*)* There's no other
way. I believe this thing knows that I plan to protect
Miss Lucy. This will put it on its guard and the
first moment she is alone it will no doubt try to get
at her, for a vampire must have blood or its life in
death ceases.

HARKER. No, I forbid this.

SEWARD. She's my daughter, and I consent. We'll
show the Professor he's mistaken.

HARKER. You allow it only because you don't believe, and I do believe. My God, Doctor, I've heard
that lunatic laugh—life-eating, you said he was, and
you subject Lucy to that risk.

VAN HELSING. *(Interrupting harshly)* I must be
master here or I can do nothing. I must know in

what form this Thing comes before I can plan how to stamp it out. Bring your daughter here. *(Crosses L. as SEWARD goes up; turns and sees HARKER looking at him; stares at HARKER. There is a short pause, then HARKER reluctantly exits C. SEWARD exits C. VAN HELSING puts back chair by desk; thinks a moment; stands C. He turns R., then L., noting the positions of doors, furniture, etc. He then crosses and turns out LIGHTS. The room is dark except for the firelight. VAN HELSING moves into firelight, looks at divan, then walks back to door C., and turns, looking at couch, satisfying himself that the light from the fire is sufficient to see anything that happens on the divan. Opens curtains. Doors C. open sharply and VAN HELSING starts violently and the ATTENDANT enters, crosses down R. and up C.)*

ATTENDANT. Beg pardon, sir. Is Doctor Seward here?

VAN HELSING. What do you want with him?

ATTENDANT. Ole Flycatcher's escaped again, sir.

VAN HELSING. Escaped, how?

ATTENDANT. Gor' blimme, cut of the window. The door's still locked and I was in the corridor all the while. It's a drop of thirty feet to the stone flagging. That loonie's a bloomin' flyin' squirrel 'e is.

VAN HELSING. *(Commandingly)* Say nothing to Doctor Seward at present. Nothing, do you hear? Now go. *(ATTENDANT exits. VAN HELSING switches on LIGHTS again; crosses R. and down to below divan. Enter LUCY C., supported by HARKER and SEWARD. HARKER is on her R.)*

LUCY. Oh! Oh!

SEWARD. Lucy, you have nothing to fear. *(They take her to divan.)*

VAN HELSING. I want you to lie down here, my dear.

LUCY. But, Doctor——

VAN HELSING. You trust me, do you not? *(She smiles weakly at him; nods. They place her on divan. VAN HELSING puts pillow R. under her head. SEWARD, at L. end of couch, arranges her skirt. HARKER back of divan.)* I want you to lie here for just a little.

LUCY. But—I am so frightened.

VAN HELSING. Make your mind passive. Try not to think. Sleep if you can.

LUCY. I dare not sleep. It is when I sleep—— *(HARKER takes her hand.)*   *(WARN Curtain.)*

VAN HELSING. *(Arranging her on couch, head on pillows, soothingly)* I know, my dear. I know. I am going to cure you, with God's help.

LUCY. Oh, but, Father.

SEWARD. You must do as the Professor says. Come, Harker.

VAN HELSING. Come, Harker. *(VAN HELSING motions out SEWARD; steps to C. door. HARKER hovers over LUCY. Exit C. SEWARD. HARKER lingers and VAN HELSING calls him. HARKER crosses up and exits. VAN HELSING pats him on back as he and HARKER go out. VAN HELSING switches off LIGHTS. No movement. LUCY closes her eyes. Low HOWL is heard outside—howl of a wolf. It is followed by a distant BARKING of dogs. FIRE-LIGHT grows dimmer. DRACULA's hand appears from back of couch, then his face. LUCY screams; swoons. When LUCY screams, AD LIB off stage up C. until VAN HELSING switches on LIGHTS.)*

HARKER. Lucy! Lucy!

SEWARD. Professor, what is it?

(Panel should be opened in wall bookcase after LIGHTS are switched out. DRACULA, who crawls on all fours, comes out of panel in dark, and scampers back into panel when VAN HELSING throws doors open. The panel closes a sec-

ond before VAN HELSING *switches on LIGHTS.
The effect here depends on speed of business.
VAN HELSING enters L.; switches on LIGHTS.
SEWARD is on his L. HARKER L. of SEWARD.
They stand just in front of door* C. *as a* BAT
flies in the room from window to C., *then out
of the window.* BAT *comes in the second the
LIGHTS are on.)*

VAN HELSING. *(Crosses down* R. *to below sofa)*
You saw?

SEWARD. God, what was that?

HARKER. Lucy, Lucy, speak to me.

VAN HELSING. Take her to her room, Harker,
quickly. (HARKER *carries* LUCY *up to* R. *of door* C.
as DRACULA *enters* C.; *walks down stage three steps;
looks about, his glance taking in* EVERYONE.)

DRACULA. *(Mildly, sympathetically)* The patient
is better, I hope?

(RENFIELD *gives a wild laugh off stage* R. VAN HEL-
SING, SEWARD *and* HARKER *look* R. RENFIELD
gives a second wild laugh.)

CURTAIN

ACT TWO

SCENE: LUCY'S *boudoir. Window* R. *rear, closed but curtains open. Chairs, small occasional table with toilet articles on it by window,* R. *Couch against wall up* L.C. *Mirror on wall* L. *Small stand, with flowers in vase, near wall* L. *Doors,* R., *leading into bedroom,* L. *leading into hall. Arch* L.C.

TIME: *The next evening.*

AT RISE: *Dogs HOWLING. As Curtain rises,* MAID *enters door* R., *steps in doorway, glances up at window over her left shoulder, takes a few steps* C., *looks back over right shoulder, then to couch and takes newspaper. Sits on couch; reads newspaper. As she turns a page,* ATTENDANT *knocks on door* L.

MAID. *(Starts—on couch* C.*)* Who is that?

ATTENDANT. *(Enters, in uniform, at door* L. *He smiles at her)* Excuse me, Miss. Did you 'appen to 'ave seen anything of the Guv'ner's pet looney? 'E's out again, 'e is.

MAID. *(Holding paper)* And what would he be doing here? You'll not hold your job, you won't, if you can't keep that man safe and sound. Why, he gets out every night. *(Crosses toward door* R.*)*

ATTENDANT. 'Ere, don't go, Miss.

MAID. Miss Lucy's asked for the evening paper. *(*ATTENDANT *crosses up* L. *and looks about room.*

MAID *smiles as she goes off* R.; *indicates speedy return.* ATTENDANT *looks out of window and then looks under couch.* MAID *returns. Her line comes just as* ATTENDANT *bends over, causing him to jump back, frightened)* Well, have you found him? *(Crosses to dresser.)*

ATTENDANT. No, I 'aven't. *(Confidentially)* And I'll tell you, Miss, this job is fair gettin' on my nerves.

MAID. Your nerves? *(Crosses to down* R.C.) And what about my nerves? Isn't it enough to have dogs howling every night and foreign counts bobbing up out of the floor, and Miss Lucy taking on the way she does, with everybody having their veins drained of blood for her, and this Dutch Sherlock Holmes with the X-ray eyes about, without you letting that Renfield loose?

ATTENDANT. *(*L.C. *Grieved)* I 'aven't let 'im loose. *(Steps up* L.) Just now I 'ears a noise like a wolf 'owling. I opens 'is door with me key, and what do I see but 'is legs goin' through the window as though 'e was goin' to climb down that smooth wall. 'E ain't 'uman, 'e ain't.

MAID. Climb down the wall?

ATTENDANT. *(Gloomily)* I don't expect no one to believe it, but I seen it, and w'ot's more, I grabbed 'old of 'is feet, I did.

MAID. *(Laughs unbelievingly)* Climbing down, head first, like a bat?

ATTENDANT. Queer your mention o bats, for just as I got 'old of 'im, a bit bat flies in the window and 'its me in the face.

MAID. *(Mysteriously)* I know where that bat came from.

ATTENDANT. *(Startled)* You do? Where?

MAID. Out of your belfry. *(Crosses to head of couch and arranges pillows, then to dresser.)*

ATTENDANT. No, Miss, it's Gawd's truth I'm tell-in' yer—*(Look from her)* —out that bat flies, and the looney is gone, but I 'eard 'im laugh, and Gawd, what a laugh. Blimme, but I'll catch it from the Guv'ner for this.

MAID. *(At dressing table)* If you tell the Governor any such tales he'll shut you up with the looney.

ATTENDANT. Lor', miss, but you're a smart one— that's just what I've been thinkin', and I daren't tell 'im what I see or what I 'eard. But 'e's 'armless, this bloke.

MAID. *(Ironically)* Wouldn't hurt a fly, would he? *(Crosses R.)*

ATTENDANT. 'Urt a fly? Oh, no, not 'e. 'E only eats 'em. Why, 'e'd rather eat a few blue-bottles than a pound of the best steak, and what 'e does to spiders is a crime.

MAID. It seems to me somebody will be coming after you in a minute, you and your spiders.

ATTENDANT. *(Crosses up R.)* I say, Miss. This is a queer neighborhood. *(Stands looking out of window up R.)* What a drop that is to the ground. *(Turns to her)* You don't have to be afraid of burglars, do you? No way of getting up here unless they fly. *(Crosses to C.)* Don't you never feel a bit lonesome like, out there—*(Points to window)* —on your nights off?

MAID. Just lately I have a bit. *(Looks toward window and crosses few steps C.)* I never noticed trees had such shadows before.

ATTENDANT. Well—if you feel you'd like a h'escort, Miss——

MAID. I'll not walk with you in your uniform. People might be taking me for one of your loonies.

ATTENDANT. *(Puts arm around her)* In mufti, then, tomorrow night.

MAID. I say, you haven't wasted much time, have you?

ATTENDANT. I've 'ad my eye on you.

MAID. Better keep that eye on your looney, or you'll be looking for a new job. (ATTENDANT *tries to kiss her. She pushes him off and slaps him*) Here, you. Buzz off. Your Guvernor will be in any minute. *(Gestures to door L.)* Go find your looney.

ATTENDANT. Oh, orl right, but I've got somethin' 'ere that'll tempt 'im back to 'is room.

MAID. Why, what's that? *(He fumbles in pocket. She comes up to him.)*

ATTENDANT. *(Takes white mouse by tail out of pocket; holds it in her face)* This 'ere.

MAID. *(Screams; crosses* R.; *climbs on chair; holds skirts)* Take it away! Take it away!

ATTENDANT. *(*MOUSE *climbs up his arm to shoulder. To* MOUSE*)* Come on, Cuthbert. We ain't too popular. *(Offended, walks off* L. *with dignity, remarking from door)* Some people 'ave *no* sense of humor.

SEWARD. *(Enters hastily from bedroom* R.; *crosses to* C.*)* What was that?

MAID. *(Puts down her skirts)* Pardon, sir. He frightened me with that—that animal.

SEWARD. *(Agitated)* Animal, what animal?

MAID. A white mouse, sir.

SEWARD. *(Relieved)* You mustn't scream—not in this house—*now.*

MAID. I'm sorry, sir, but that nasty little beast—

SEWARD. You alarmed Miss Lucy so. She's dreadfully upset as it is by something in the paper.

MAID. Oh, do you mean about that Hampstead Horror, sir? The lady in white who gives chocolates to little children——

SEWARD. *(Interrupts impatiently)* Never mind that, but I will not have Miss Lucy disturbed. *(Exits* R. *DOGS howl until* DRACULA *speaks.* MAID *crosses* L.; *looks toward window, then crosses* L. *LIGHTS go out.* MAID *screams. GREEN SPOT comes on*

DRACULA. *He has entered at window up* R. *while lights are out. When GREEN SPOT comes on he is* R.C. MAID *screams again as she sees him.)*

DRACULA. *(Soothingly, his English perfect but his accent foreign)* Forgive me. My footfall is not heavy, and your rugs are soft.

MAID. *(Crossing slowly* R.*)* It's all right, sir— but how did you come in?

DRACULA. *(Smiling)* The door of this room was ajar, so I did not knock. How is Miss Lucy and her nervous prostration?

MAID. *(On a direct line with* DRACULA*)* I think she's better, sir.

DRACULA. Ah, good. But the strain of Miss Lucy's illness has made you also ill.

MAID. How did you know, sir? But it's only a pain in my head that runs down into the neck.

DRACULA. *(Winningly)* I can remove this pain.

MAID. I don't understand, sir.

DRACULA. Such pains yield readily to suggestion.

MAID. *(Raises arm slightly to shield herself)* Excuse me, sir, but if it's hypnotism you mean, I'd rather have the pain.

DRACULA. *(Winningly)* Ah, you think of hypnotism as an ugly waving of arms and many passes. That is not my method. *(As he speaks he gestures quietly with his left hand and she stares at him, fascinated. Placing his left thumb against her forehead, he stares straight into her eyes. She makes feeble effort to remove his hand, then remains quiescent and he now speaks coldly, imperatively; turns her face front before speaking)* What is given can be taken away. From now on you have no pain. And you have no will of your own. Do you hear me?

MAID. *(Murmurs)* I hear you.

DRACULA. When you awake you will not remember what I say. Doctor Seward ordered you today to sleep with your mistress every night in the same bed because of her bad dreams. Is it not so?

MAID. *(Murmurs)* Yes, Master.

DRACULA. Your mistress is threatened by horror and by death, but I will save her. A man whose will is at cross purposes with mine has come to this house. I will crush him. Receive your orders. You hear me?

MAID. Yes, Master.

DRACULA. Hear and obey. From now on you will carry out any suggestion that reaches you from my brain instantly without question. When I will you to do a thing it shall be done. My call will reach you soon. *(GREEN SPOT dims out slowly. DRACULA exits through window. LIGHTS come on. DOGS howl outside until VAN HELSING enters L. MAID looks up at window, then to L.; takes a step or two R. as VAN HELSING enters. She starts when door shuts.)*

VAN HELSING. *(Enters L. His face is paler. He looks drawn and weak. He carries box tied with string. Crosses to R.C.)* You've not left your mistress alone?

MAID. Doctor Seward is with her, sir. *(Sways a little.)*

VAN HELSING. *(Looking at her keenly)* What's wrong with you, my girl?

MAID. Nothing, sir.

VAN HELSING. You've just had a severe shock.

MAID. It's nothing, sir. I—I suddenly felt queer. *(Looks toward window)* That's all. I can't remember anything.

VAN HELSING. Mr. Harker has just arrived. Ask Doctor Seward to come here. Remain with Miss Lucy yourself.

MAID. Yes, sir. *(Crosses R.)* She's dreadfully upset, sir.

VAN HELSING. Upset over what?

MAID. It's in the evening paper, sir. About the Hampstead Horror. (VAN HELSING *motions* MAID *to silence.*) Yes, sir.

VAN HELSING. *(Shaken)* Oh, God, she has seen it. *(Exit* MAID R. *Enter* HARKER L.*)*

HARKER. *(In doorway* L.*, worried)* Everything just the same? (VAN HELSING *nods.* HARKER *closes door)* When I leave this house even for a few hours I dread what I—— *(Steps* R. *to* C.*)* I dread what I may find when I come back.

VAN HELSING. And well you may, my friend. *(Places box on table under mirror* L.*)*

HARKER. God must have sent you here to help us. Without you there'd be no hope. And this morning, Professor, when you opened your veins to revive Lucy again——

VAN HELSING. It was the least I could do—for my lack of foresight was responsible for this attack.

HARKER. Don't say that.

VAN HELSING. Her maid slept with her—and yet we found the wolf's-bane thrown off the bed to the floor.

HARKER. She was so weak, so pale, the two little wounds opened fresh again——

VAN HELSING. *(With gesture to box)* I have prepared a stronger defense. But our main task is not defense, but attack. What have you found in London? *(Steps to* C.*)*

HARKER. A lot, but Heaven knows what it means or whether it's any use.

VAN HELSING. I, too, have had news of which I can make nothing.

SEWARD. *(Enters* R.*; crosses to* R.C. *To* HARKER*)* Ah, John, back from town.

HARKER. Yes. *(Sits* L. *end of couch.)*

VAN HELSING. We must try to piece together what we have learned today. *(Producing telegram of several sheets)* My colleague in Bucharest wires that the Dracula family has been extinct—for five hundred years.

SEWARD. Can the Count be an impostor?

VAN HELSING. *(Referring to telegram)* The castle he calls his own is a desolate ruin near the border. It was built, as you said, Harker, by the terrible Voivode Dracula, who was said to have had dealings with evil spirits. He was the last of his race. But for many generations the peasants have believed the castle Dracula inhabited by a vampire.

HARKER. Then it must be he——

VAN HELSING. *(Shakes head; puts telegram back in pocket)* My friends, I am bewildered.

SEWARD. But surely this confirms your suspicions. I was incredulous till I saw that creature hovering over Lucy——

VAN HELSING. A vampire from Transylvania cannot be in England.

SEWARD. But why?

VAN HELSING. Because, as I have told you, the vampire must rest by day in the earth in which the corpse it inhabits was buried.

HARKER. *(Excited)* In the earth. *(Rises.)*

VAN HELSING. The vampire must return to its burial place by sunrise.

HARKER. *(Excited)* I found today that Dracula arrived at the Croydon airdrome in a three-engined German plane, on March sixth.

SEWARD. March the sixth? Three days before Mina first was taken ill.

HARKER. This plane had made a non-stop flight from Sekely in Transylvania. It left just after sunset. It arrived two hours before dawn. It carried only the Count and six packing cases. .

VAN HELSING. Did you learn what was in those cases?

HARKER. He told the Customs people he wanted

to see whether Transylvania plants would grow in a foreign climate in their native soil.

VAN HELSING. Soil? What was in those boxes? *(Steps down L.)*

HARKER. Just plain dirt. He left in a lorry, with the six coffin-like boxes, before sunrise.

VAN HELSING. Oh, God, yes, before sunrise. The King of Vampires, my friends. *(Crosses between SEWARD and HARKER)* This creature is the terrible Voivode Dracula himself. In his satanic pride and contempt, he even uses his own name. For who could suspect? For five hundred years he has been fettered to his castle because he must sleep by day in his graveyard. Five centuries pass. The aeroplane is invented. His chance has come, for now he can cross Europe in a single night. He prepared six coffins filled with the earth in which he must rest by day. He leaves his castle after sunset. By dawn he is in London and safe in one of his cases—a great risk, but he has triumphed. He has reached London with its teeming millions, with its "opportunity," as he said——

SEWARD. God protect my Lucy. *(Crosses R. a few steps and back.)*

HARKER. *(To VAN HELSING, new tone)* I saw the estate agent from whom he bought Carfax here and got the address of four old houses he has leased in different parts of London.

VAN HELSING. One of his coffin retreats is in each of those houses.

SEWARD. Two heavy boxes were delivered at Carfax the day after he took possession.

VAN HELSING. He has scattered them, for safety. If we can find all six, we can destroy him.

SEWARD. But how?

VAN HELSING. His native earth will no longer receive his unclean form if each box is sanctified with holy water.

HARKER. Then we must get at those boxes, tear them open one by one. If we find him, then in God's name, Professor, I demand that my hand shall drive the stake into this devil's heart and send his soul to hell! (SEWARD *motions no noise because of* LUCY.)

VAN HELSING. Your plan is too dangerous.

SEWARD. But why? These attacks on Lucy continue. Are we to delay while my child is dying?

HARKER. No, not for a moment.

VAN HELSING. Patience, my friends. This creature is more than mortal. His cunning is the growth of the ages. How if we find five of his boxes and close them against him, and cannot find the sixth?

SEWARD. Well?

VAN HELSING. Then he will bury himself in his last refuge, where we can never find him and sleep until we are all dead.

HARKER. Then Lucy will be safe.

VAN HELSING. For her life, yes—but his unclean kiss has claimed her for his own. When she dies she will become as he is, a foul thing of the night. The vampire can wait. No, my friends, there is only one way to save her from him—to destroy him.

SEWARD. You're right, as always.

VAN HELSING. We have one great advantage—by day he is a coffined corpse—of our search by day he can know nothing, if we leave no traces.

HARKER. God, this delay. *(Move to window.)*

VAN HELSING. We must make the round of his houses and find all six boxes, without his knowledge, and *then* we act.

SEWARD. But what about the caretakers or servants? (HARKER *crosses down* R.)

VAN HELSING. All the houses will be empty. The vampire plays a lone hand. *(Maniacal LAUGH heard behind curtains of window* R. SEWARD *crosses to window.* HARKER *steps up and faces window and then comes down* R.)

SEWARD. Renfield! *(Takes* RENFIELD *by arm and throws him into room* R.C. RENFIELD *laughs cunningly.)*

VAN HELSING. He's been here all the time we've been talking.

SEWARD. Did you hear what we were saying, man?

RENFIELD. Yes, I heard—something—enough— *(With gestures to* SEWARD *and* HARKER*)* Be guided by what he says. *(Points to* VAN HELSING. *To* SEWARD*)* It is your only hope——— *(To* HARKER*)* It is her only hope. *(Crosses to* VAN HELSING*)* It is *my* only hope. *(Falls on knees before* VAN HELSING*)* Save my soul! Save my soul! I am weak. You are strong. I am crazy. You are sane. You are good and he is evil.

VAN HELSING. *(Impressively)* I will save you, Renfield, but you must tell me what you know. Everything.

RENFIELD. *(Rises)* Know? What should I know? I don't know anything. *(Taps head)* You say I'm mad and Doctor Seward will tell you about that. You mustn't pay any attention to anything I say.

SEWARD. *(Stepping down)* We can't waste time with this fellow. I'll have him taken away. *(Crosses* R. *to bell ring; returns two steps up* L.)

RENFIELD. *(Gets up—to* SEWARD*)* Fool, fool, and I thought you were wise. The whole world is mad just now, and if you want help you must come to a madman to get it. *(Little laugh cunningly)* But I'll not give it to you, I'm afraid. *(Turns to window)* A wise madman will obey him who is strong and not the weak.

VAN HELSING. *(Steps to him fiercely)* Him? Whom do you mean?

RENFIELD. Need we mention names among

friends? Come, Professor, be reasonable. What
have I got to gain by being on your side? The Doctor keeps me shut up all day, and if I'm good he
gives me a little sugar to spread out for my flies, but
on the other hand, if I serve him—— *(Points to
window up* R.*)*

VAN HELSING. *(Sharply, taking him by coat)*
The blood is the life, eh, Renfield? *(Dragging him
again)* What have you to do with Count Dracula?

RENFIELD. *(Convulsed with terror)* Dracula.
(Drawing himself up defiantly) I never even heard
the name before.

VAN HELSING. You are lying.

RENFIELD. Madmen, Professor, lack the power to
discriminate between truth and falsehood—*(Breaks
away)* —so I take no offence at what most men
would consider an affront. *(Crosses to* SEWARD;
kneels L. *of* SEWARD*)* Send me away. I asked you
to before and you wouldn't. If you only knew what
has happened since then. I dare not tell you more.
I dare not. I should die in torment if I betrayed—

VAN HELSING. *(Crosses a step* R.*)* Doctor Seward will send you away if you speak.

SEWARD. Yes, Renfield. (RENFIELD *moans.)* I
offer you your soul in exchange for what you
know.

RENFIELD. *(Rises)* God will not damn a poor
lunatic's soul. God knows the devil is too strong
for us who have weak minds. But send me away—
I want you to promise, Doctor Seward.

SEWARD. If you will speak.

VAN HELSING. Come, Renfield.

RENFIELD. *(Pause. Sets himself; looks at* SEW-
ARD, VAN HELSING, HARKER *and* SEWARD *again,
then speaks as a sane man)* Then I will tell you.
Count Dracula is—— (BAT *comes in window; flies
out again.* RENFIELD *rushes to window with arms
outstretched, screaming)* Master. Master, I didn't

say anything. I told them nothing. I'm loyal to you. I am your slave. *(The* OTHERS *rush to window.* SEWARD *and* HARKER *first.* VAN HELSING *goes but a few steps up.)*

SEWARD. *(Looking out window)* There's a big bat flying in a circle. It's gone.

HARKER. What's that, just passing that small shrub? It looks like a big grey dog.

VAN HELSING. Are you sure it was a dog?

HARKER. *(Steps down)* Well, it might easily be a wolf. Oh, but that's nonsense. Our nerves are making us see things.

VAN HELSING. Come, Renfield. What were you about to say?

RENFIELD. Nothing, nothing. *(Moves down.* LUCY *enters* R. *with newspaper; crosses* R.C. *to* VAN HELSING.)

LUCY. Professor—have you seen what's in this—

VAN HELSING. Miss Lucy, give it to——

RENFIELD. *(Crosses down to her)* Are you Miss Seward?

LUCY. I am. (SEWARD *moves to above her; indicates* HARKER *to ring bell.)*

RENFIELD. *(Crosses down to her as she turns)* Then in the name of the merciful and compassionate God, leave this place at once. *(She turns to him.* VAN HELSING *motions silence to* OTHERS.)

LUCY. But this is my home. Nothing would induce me to leave.

RENFIELD. *(Sane)* Oh, that's true. You wouldn't go if they tried to drag you away, would you? It's too late. What a fool I am. I shall be punished for this and it can't do any good. It's too late. *(In tone of pity)* You are so young, so beautiful, so pure. Even I have decent feelings sometimes, and I must tell you, and if you don't go your soul will pay for it. You're in the power of—— (BAT *flies in window and out.* RENFIELD *to window and screams.*

SEWARD *swings* L. *toward couch.* HARKER *crosses to* LUCY *to protect her.)* The Master is at hand. *(Crosses* L. *on knees.* ATTENDANT *appears door* L.*)*

SEWARD. Butterworth! (SEWARD *helps* REN-FIELD *up, then* ATTENDANT *grasps him and takes him to* L. *door.)*

RENFIELD. *(At door)* Goodbye, Miss Seward. Since you will not heed my warning, I pray God that I may never see your face again. *(Exits* L. *with* ATTENDANT.*)*

LUCY. What did he mean, Professor? What did he mean? Why did he say that? *(Exiting* R. *in hysterics.* HARKER *follows her.)*

SEWARD. That crazy thing in league with the devil; horrible, and Lucy already upset by something in the paper.

VAN HELSING. Go in and get that paper from her.

SEWARD. *(Step* R.*)* Whatever it is, she keeps on reading that article again and again.

VAN HELSING. Take it away from her, man, and come back to me. *(Places hand on forehead as if faint.)*

SEWARD. *(Turns at door* R.*)* Don't overdo it, Van Helsing. God knows where we should be if you went under. After a transfusion operation, at your age you really ought to be in bed—the loss of so much blood is serious.

VAN HELSING. I never felt more fit in my life.

SEWARD. I only ask you not to overestimate your strength now, when we lean on you—— *(As he exits* R. *he points to mirror)* Feeling fit, are you? Just look at yourself in the glass.

(VAN HELSING, *alone, registers as tired and ex-hausted, and walks slowly across room, looking at his drawn face in mirror* L. DRACULA, *with stealthy tread, in evening dress and cloak as*

before, enters from window up R. *and walks
slowly to directly behind* VAN HELSING.)

VAN HELSING. *(Looking at himself, touching
face, shakes head)* The devil.

DRACULA. Come. (VAN HELSING *turns suddenly
to him and looks back into the mirror.)* Not as bad
as that. *(Suave, cold, ironical.)*

VAN HELSING. *(Long look in mirror, then turns
to* DRACULA. *Controlling himself with difficulty)*
I did not hear you, Count.

DRACULA. I am often told that I have a light
footstep.

VAN HELSING. I was looking in the mirror.
(Turns and looks again; turns back to DRACULA)
It's reflection covers the whole room, but I cannot
see—— *(Pause. Turns to mirror.* DRACULA, *face
convulsed by fury, picks up small vase with flowers
from stand, smashes mirror, pieces of mirror and
vase tumbling to floor.* VAN HELSING *steps back;
looks at* DRACULA *with loathing and terror.)*

DRACULA. *(Recovering composure)* Forgive me,
I dislike mirrors. They are the playthings of man's
vanity. *(Down* R.C.) And how's the fair patient?

VAN HELSING. *(Meaningly)* The diagnosis presents difficulties.

DRACULA. I feared it might, my friend.

VAN HELSING. Would you care to see what I
have prescribed for my patient?

DRACULA. Anything that you prescribe for Miss
Lucy has the greatest interest for me. (VAN HEL-
SING *crosses to table under mirror to get box.*
DRACULA *crosses* L.; *meets* VAN HELSING *coming
back with box.* VAN HELSING *deliberately turns
back on him, causing* DRACULA *to cross, circling
down* L. VAN HELSING *goes to small table at* R. *of
arch* L. VAN HELSING *turns front as he opens pocket*

knife, then turns to cut string on box he has placed on table. As he turns upstage DRACULA faces upstage. VAN HELSING, in cutting string of parcel on table L., cuts his finger. VAN HELSING gives slight exclamation of pain; holds up finger covered with blood. DRACULA starts for VAN HELSING with right hand raised, then keeping control with difficulty, turns away so as not to see blood. VAN HELSING stares at him a moment, then walks up and sticks bleeding finger in front of him.)

VAN HELSING. The prescription is a most unusual one. *(DRACULA, baring teeth, makes sudden snap at finger. VAN HELSING turns away quickly; ties handkerchief around it. DRACULA again regains poise with an effort.)*

DRACULA. The cut is not deep—I—looked.

VAN HELSING. *(Opening parcel)* No, but it will serve. Here is my medicine for Miss Lucy. *(DRACULA comes up to VAN HELSING, who quickly holds handful of wolf's-bane up to his face. DRACULA leaps back, face distorted with rage and distress, shielding himself with cloak. Putting wolf's-bane back in box)* You do not care for the smell? *(VAN HELSING backs to R.C.)*

DRACULA. You are a wise man, Professor—for one who has not lived even a single lifetime.

VAN HELSING. You flatter me, Count.

DRACULA. But not wise enough to return to Holland at once, now that you have learned what you have learned. *(Crosses two steps R.)*

VAN HELSING. *(Shortly)* I preferred to remain. *(Meaningly)* Even though a certain lunatic here attempted to kill me.

DRACULA. *(Smiling)* Lunatics are difficult. They do not do what they are told. They even try to betray their benefactors. But when servants fail to obey orders, the Master must carry them out for himself.

Van Helsing. *(Grimly)* I anticipated as much.

Dracula. *(Step* L., *gazing at him intently)* In the past five hundred years, Professor, those who have crossed my path have all died, and some not pleasantly. *(Continues to gaze at* Van Helsing; *lifts his arm slowly; says with terrible emphasis and force)* Come—here. *(*Van Helsing *pales, staggers, then slowly takes three steps toward* Dracula. *Very slight pause as* Van Helsing *attempts to regain control of himself, then takes another step toward* Dracula—*pauses, places hand to brow, then completely regains control of himself and looks away to* R.C.*)* Ah, your will is strong. Then I must come to you. *(Advances to* Van Helsing, *who takes out of breast pocket small velvet bag.* Dracula *stops)* More medicine, Professor?

Van Helsing. More effective than wolf's-bane, Count.

Dracula. Indeed? *(Starts for* Van Helsing's *throat.* Van Helsing *holds bag out toward him.* Dracula's *face becomes convulsed with terror and he retreats* L. *before* Van Helsing, *who follows him.)* Sacrilege.

Van Helsing. *(Continuing to advance)* I have a dispensation. *(*Van Helsing *has cut him off from the door* L. *and remorselessly presses him toward window* R. Dracula, *livid with rage and snarling, backs out of the window. As* Dracula *is just outside the window he spreads his cape like a bat and gives a long satirical laugh as he makes exit.* Van Helsing *almost collapses; puts bag back in pocket; crosses himself; mops perspiration from brow with handkerchief. A SHOT is heard.* Van Helsing *leaps up; rushes to window.* Bat *circles almost into his face. He staggers back.* Seward *hurries in, carrying newspaper, from door* R.*)*

Seward. God, Van Helsing, what was that? *(Dropping newspaper on table.)*

VAN HELSING. A revolver shot. It came as a relief. That at least is something human.

SEWARD. Who broke the mirror? *(Enter* HARKER R.)

VAN HELSING. I.

HARKER. Sorry if I startled you. I saw that infernal bat around this side of the house. I couldn't resist a shot.

SEWARD. Did you hit it?

HARKER. Why, I——

VAN HELSING. The bullet was never made, my friend, that could harm *that* bat. *My* weapons are stronger.

HARKER. What do you mean?

VAN HELSING. Dracula has been here.

SEWARD. *(A step down* R.*)* Good God!

HARKER. How did he get in?

VAN HELSING. You ask how the Vampire King, during the hours of night, the hours that are his, comes and goes? As the wind, my friend, as he pleases. He came to kill me. *(Puts hand on breast)* But I carry a power stronger than his.

HARKER. What power?

VAN HELSING. I expected an attack. I secured a dispensation from the Cardinal. I have with me— *(Crosses himself)* —the Host. (HARKER *crosses himself.)* He came. I proved my case if it needed proof. The mirror does not reflect this *man that was,* who casts no shadow. See, I cut my finger, *it* leapt at the blood, but before the sacred wafer *it* fled.

SEWARD. Lucy must not know.

VAN HELSING. *(Gently, worried)* Miss Lucy knows—more than you think.

HARKER. How can she? If she knew, she'd tell me.

VAN HELSING. As these attacks continue she comes more and more under his power. There is a

mystic link between them. (SEWARD *sighs.*) Oh, it
is hard to bear, but you must face it. It may be
that he can already learn what passes in her mind.
And so Miss Lucy must not be told that we know
about earth boxes—for he may learn—whatever she
knows. (LUCY *enters* R.)

SEWARD. But Professor, that would mean that
Lucy is in collusion with this creature. That's impossible—— (LUCY *crosses to dresser; takes news-*
paper.)

VAN HELSING. No, no, Miss Lucy, you must not.
(LUCY *crosses to* R. *of* VAN HELSING.)

HARKER. Lucy, what's in this paper that's upset
you?

LUCY. (*Hands newspaper to* HARKER) Read it.
John. (HARKER *takes newspaper; reads.* VAN HEL-
SING *moves as if to stop him, then checks himself.*)

VAN HELSING. No, Harker, no. (*Backs to* L. *of*
couch.)

LUCY. Read it! (LUCY *sits on couch. They* ALL
listen. SEWARD *crosses down to* R. *of* HARKER.)

HARKER. (*Reading*) "The Hampstead Horror.
Further attacks on small children, committed after
dark by a mysterious and beautiful woman in Hampstead, are reported today. Narratives of three small
girls, all under ten years of age, tally in essential
details. Each child speaks of a beautiful lady in
white who gave her chocolates, enticed her to some
secluded corner and there kissed and fondled her
and bit her slightly in the throat." (*Looks at* SEW-
ARD *and* LUCY; *drops paper to side.*)

LUCY. Go on.

HARKER. (*Reading*) "The wounds are trivial.
The children suffered no other harm and do not
seem to have been frightened. Indeed, one small girl
told her mother she hoped she might see the beautiful lady again." (*Turns to* LUCY. SEWARD *takes*
paper from HARKER.)

VAN HELSING. So soon—so soon. (HARKER *and* SEWARD *look at each other.*)

SEWARD. You know what has been happening, Lucy? (LUCY *nods.*)

HARKER. Professor Van Helsing knows, too, Lucy, and he knows how to protect you.

LUCY. Is it not too late?

VAN HELSING. No, Miss Lucy, it is not too late.

SEWARD. These poor innocent children——

VAN HELSING. *(Crosses to foot of couch. To* SEWARD*)* You think Count Dracula—— (LUCY *shudders.*)

LUCY. Not that name.

VAN HELSING. You think the Werewolf has done this too?

SEWARD. Of course, in the form of a woman. Who else could it be?

VAN HELSING. It is worse. Far worse.

HARKER. Worse? What do you mean? (LUCY *motionless, her face frozen in horror.*)

VAN HELSING. Miss Lucy knows.

LUCY. The woman in white—is Mina.

HARKER. Mina. But she's dead, Lucy.

LUCY. She has joined—the Master.

SEWARD. Oh, God, have pity on us all. *(Drops newspaper on chair* R.*)*

VAN HELSING. My dear Miss Lucy, I will not ask you how you know. After tonight no more little children will meet the woman in white. She will remain at rest—in the tomb where you laid her. And her soul, released from this horror, will be with God.

LUCY. How can you do this?

VAN HELSING. Do not ask me.

LUCY. *(Takes hold of* VAN HELSING's *arm)* Professor, if you can save Mina's soul after her death, can you save mine?

HARKER. Oh, Lucy! *(Sitting above her, on couch, arm around her.)*

VAN HELSING. *(Takes her hand)* I will save you. In God's name, I swear it. And He has given me a sign—in this room tonight.

LUCY. Then promise me one thing. Whatever you plan to do, whatever you know, do not tell me. *(Turns to HARKER)* Not even if I beg you to tell me, swear that you will not, now, while I am still yours, while I am myself, promise it.

HARKER. I promise it. *(Takes her in his arms; tries to kiss her.)*

LUCY. *(Breaks from him, horrified)* No, no, John. You mustn't kiss me. Promise that you never will, not even if I beg you to.

HARKER. I promise.

VAN HELSING. My dear Miss Lucy, from tonight on one of us will be awake all night, here in this room, next to your bedroom, with your door open.

LUCY. *(Murmurs)* You are so good.

VAN HELSING. Yes, and I will make the room safe for you. Your maid will be with you. (HARKER *talks to* LUCY *on couch while* VAN HELSING *takes handful of wolf's-bane.)* Doctor, rub these over the window in the little room there. See, like this. *(He starts rubbing around edge of window up* R.) Rub it around the sashes and especially above the lock. (SEWARD *watches* VAN HELSING *rubbing, then takes wolf's-bane from* VAN HELSING *quickly, crosses* L. *and out through arch up* L.C. VAN HELSING *turns, goes to table* L. *and takes out wreath of wolf's-bane)* See, I have made this wreath that you must wear around your neck tonight. While you wear this those—dreams—cannot come to you. *(Hangs wolf's-bane around her neck. Takes out of pocket crucifix on cord, which he also hangs around her neck)* Swear to me that you will not take these off.

LUCY. I promise.

VAN HELSING. Swear it on the cross.

LUCY. *(Kisses cross)* I swear it. (VAN HELSING *crosses toward door* L.)

HARKER. *(Crosses to* R. *of* VAN HELSING*)* Professor, surely the Host is more powerful than this wolfe's-bane.

VAN HELSING. Of course.

HARKER. Then leave the Host with her—nothing can harm her then.

VAN HELSING. No, the Host cannot be used where there has been pollution. *(SCREAMS off* L.*)* What is it? (ATTENDANT *enters* L. MAID R. SEWARD *enters from arch* L.C.)

ATTENDANT. It's Renfield, sir.

SEWARD. Why haven't you got him locked up?

ATTENDANT. Because he's barred himself in, sir. He got hold of one of the patients. He had her by the throat. *(Exits* L. LUCY *rises.)*

VAN HELSING. Ah—human blood now. *(Starting* L.*)* Come, Seward. Come, Harker.

(WARN Curtain.)

SEWARD. I should have had him sent away. (MAID *crosses to* LUCY. VAN HELSING *and* SEWARD *exit* L. HARKER *hesitates, then follows them off* L. HARKER *ad libs. during exit,* "It's all right, Lucy. I'll be right back," *etc.)*

LUCY. John—— *(To* MAID*)* Don't you leave me, too.

MAID. Of course I won't, Miss Lucy. It's nothing but a quarrel among the patients. Mr. Harker will be back soon. (MAID *places her on couch.* LUCY *swoons.* MAID *gets smelling salts)* Here, Miss Lucy. (DRACULA'S *face appears back of tapestry on rear wall; disappears after a count of eight or nine.* MAID *steps down* R., *face audience, gets message, then returns. Puts salts back to dresser; crosses to* LUCY*)* These evil-smelling flowers have made you faint. *(Takes crucifix and wreath, steps* R., *throws them on floor; crosses two steps down* R. *Another message comes to her. Puts hand to head, turns slowly, looks at window, steps toward couch)* It is so close, Madam. A little air—— *(Turns to window.* LUCY *moans again.* MAID *pulls back latch; opens window. As window opens, clouds of mist roll in. Steps down. Gets message. Count eight. Switches LIGHTS out. The stage is now dark. DOGS without, far and near, howl in terror.)*

(After MAID *exits* R. *DOGS continue to howl. When ALL LIGHTS out, gauze Curtain comes down and a GREEN FLOOD LIGHT dims up from front. Before green is up* DRACULA *comes on from door up* L.C. *with cape over his face. GREEN SPOT comes, covers him, and as green spot slowly dims up he brings cape down from face as he moves to* C. *ANOTHER GREEN SPOT dims up, covering the couch and* C. *of stage. He stands* C., *with back to audience, hands outstretched to resemble a large bat; moves up a few steps.* LUCY *gets up from couch slowly and falls in his arms. A long kiss and then, as she falls back on his right arm, he bares her throat and starts down to bite her as Curtain falls.)*

CURTAIN

ACT THREE

SCENE: *Scene I same as Act I.*
Empty stage. In this Act a stake and hammer are on upstage end of desk. DOGS howl until VAN HELSING *enters. A count of ten. Curtains move as if someone entering window. Then chair back of desk which is turned up stage moves around, facing front. Then* VAN HELSING *enters* C. *with* SEWARD.

VAN HELSING *pacing up and down of divan.* SEWARD *on chair* R. *of desk.* ATTENDANT *enters* C. *as* VAN HELSING *starts up stage.*

VAN HELSING. *(As* ATTENDANT *opens door)* What is it?

ATTENDANT. *(Closes door. To* VAN HELSING*)* Anybody w'ot wants my job, sir, can 'ave it. (SEWARD *rouses himself.)*

SEWARD. What's the matter?

ATTENDANT. *(Crosses two steps down)* I knows what I knows, and w'ot I seen I saw, and I 'ops it by the first train, and don't ask for no wages in loo of notice.

VAN HELSING. Where's Renfield?

ATTENDANT. If you asks me, I says 'e's probably payin' a little visit to 'ell.

SEWARD. You've let him escape again?

ATTENDANT. *(Crosses down)* Look 'ere, sir. 'Avin', so to speak, resigned, I don't 'ave to put up with any more from any of you. *(Looks at* VAN

HELSING *and* SEWARD) W'ot a man can't 'elp, 'e can't 'elp, and that's that. (SEWARD *sinks back on desk, head in hands.*)

VAN HELSING. Can't you see, man, that Doctor Seward is not well? Will you desert him when he needs all the help he can get?

ATTENDANT. Puttin' it that way, sir, I ain't the man to run under fire. But I'm sick and tired of being told off for what ain't my fault.

VAN HELSING. We don't blame you. No bolts or bars could hold Renfield.

ATTENDANT. (SEWARD *looks up at him*) Now, sir, you're talkin' sense. I 'ad 'im in a straightjacket this time. Nearly all yesterday I worked at clampin' bars across the winder. Now I finds them bars pulled apart like they was made o' cheese and 'im gone.

VAN HELSING. Then try to find him.

ATTENDANT. Find 'im, sir? Find 'im? I can't chase him up and down the wall. I ain't no bloody mountain goat! *(Exits* C.)

VAN HELSING. *(Crosses to* C.) The thing mocks us. A few hours after he finds out what we know, and what we have done, he comes here, and drags that poor creature of his to himself.

SEWARD. *(In dull, hopeless tone)* What can the vampire want with Renfield?

VAN HELSING. Renfield is serving an apprenticeship—to join the Vampire King after his death. We must prevent that.

SEWARD. What does Renfield matter? *(Moans)* If we are beaten, then there is no God.

VAN HELSING. *(Crosses to him,* L.) We dare not despair, Seward.

SEWARD. To figure out in advance what anyone would do who got on his track!

VAN HELSING. I thought we had him when we broke into Carfax and found two earth boxes there and then found one box in each of his four other houses, and when I pried up the lid of the sixth box I was sure we would find him there, helpless.

SEWARD. *(Bitterly)* Empty.

VAN HELSING. An empty packing-case, left as a blind. *(Crosses to c.)*

SEWARD. He only brought six in his plane, so there can be only the one left.

VAN HELSING. Only one, but hidden where we can never find it. And now we've put him on his guard.

SEWARD. Yes. (VAN HELSING *back to window and back to* R. *of desk. Chair turns back. Curtains flap out.* SEWARD *looks at wrist watch)* It's not half an hour till sunrise. *(Rises and crossing to fireplace.)* Poor John has been sitting up with Lucy for nine hours. She'll be safe at dawn and he can get some sleep—if anyone can sleep in this house.

VAN HELSING. Whoever else sleeps or does not sleep, Miss Lucy will sleep at dawn.

SEWARD. *(Steps* L.*)* Another horror?

VAN HELSING. Oh, you've noticed how she keeps awake all night now and sleeps by day.

SEWARD. Is that part of—the change?

VAN HELSING. Of course. And sometimes—the look that comes into her face.

SEWARD. *(Turns face away in horror)* Don't, man, for God's sake, I can't bear it!

VAN HELSING. We must face the facts, for her sake. (VAN HELSING *crosses few steps* L. *The word "suggestion" from* SEWARD *turns him back.)*

SEWARD. How could it have got at her with the wolf's-bane and the cross around her neck? *(Pause)* Suggestion, conveyed from the Monster?

VAN HELSING. Yes. He must have impelled the maid to take away the wolf's-bane and cross and open the window. I should have foreseen that. *(Crosses* R. *to* C.*)*

SEWARD. Don't blame yourself. The devil is more cunning than we are. *(Sits couch)* Yet Lucy seems better. Until this last attack she's always been exhausted, but at sunset last night, when she woke up after sleeping all day——

VAN HELSING. *(Step R.)* There was blood in her cheeks again.

SEWARD. Yes, thank God.

VAN HELSING. *(With terrible emphasis; crosses to above L. end of divan)* My poor friend, *where does that blood come from?*

SEWARD. What do you suggest now? What fresh horror—— *(Door L. opens a crack. Long skinny hand protrudes into room. SEWARD sees it first and starts in alarm. Rises. VAN HELSING turns quickly. Door opens slowly and RENFIELD slinks in.)*

RENFIELD. *(Crossing to L. of desk)* Is not half-past five in the morning a strange hour for men who aren't crazy to be up and about? *(Crosses to window.)*

VAN HELSING. *(Aside to SEWARD)* We may get help from this thing that's still half human. *(To RENFIELD)* Renfield.

RENFIELD. *(Crosses down to L.C., with growing hysteria)* He's after me. He's going to kill me.

VAN HELSING. Help us, Renfield, and we'll save you.

RENFIELD. You, you poor puny man, you measure your brains against his. You don't know what you're dealing with. You, a thick-headed Dutchman and a fool of an alienist, and a young cub of a boy. Why, not all the soldiers and police in London could stop the Master from doing as he likes.

VAN HELSING. But God can stop him.

RENFIELD. God permits evil. Why does he permit evil if He is good? Tell me that.

SEWARD. *(Stepping to R.C.)* How did you escape through those iron bars?

RENFIELD. *(Cunningly as he crosses L. to desk)* Madmen have a great strength, Doctor.

VAN HELSING. *(At L. end of divan)* Come, Renfield, we know you didn't wrench those bars apart yourself.

RENFIELD. *(Sane)* No, I didn't. I wanted them there. I hope they'd keep him out. He did it, then he called to me and I had to come. *(Crosses C., back to insanity)* The Master is angry. He promised me eternal life and live things, live things, big ones, not flies and spiders; and blood to drink, always blood. I must obey him but I don't want to be like him. *(Crosses L.)* I am mad, I know, and bad, too, for I've taken lives, but they were only little lives. I'm not like him. I wouldn't like a human life. *(LUCY laughs off stage and says, "Oh, John!" as she enters. HARKER opens and closes C. door; stands inside door. LUCY to R. of HARKER and a step down. LUCY has changed from the last Act. There is blood in her cheeks, she is stronger and seems full of vitality. She and HARKER stop in surprise at seeing RENFIELD. To LUCY)* And why did I seek to betray him? For you. *(She smiles.)* I said I'd serve the devil, but I didn't serve him honestly. I don't like women with no blood in them. *(LUCY laughs.)* And yet I warned you and made him angry, and now— *(Working into frenzy)* —perhaps he will kill me. *(LUCY laughs.)* And I won't get any more live things to eat. There'll be no more blood. *(Starts for LUCY's throat. HARKER gets him by right arm, VAN HELSING by left arm, then SEWARD steps in and takes HARKER's place as RENFIELD struggles violently. SEWARD and VAN HELSING bear him away C., struggling and screaming.)*

HARKER. Lucy, darling, you mustn't mind that poor, crazed creature.

LUCY. *(With low laugh as before)* I don't. He

amuses me. *(Crossing to divan and sitting* R. *end of it.)*

HARKER. *(Turns to window)* Oh, Lucy, how can you? The poor devil! Thank God—*(Turns to window)* —it will soon be dawn now.

LUCY. Dawn. The ebb tide of life. I hate the dawn. How can people like daylight? At night I am really alive. The night was made to enjoy life, and love—— (HARKER *turns to her; hesitates.)* Come to me, John, my own John. *(He comes and sits* L. *of her.)*

HARKER. Lucy, I'm so happy that you are better and strong again——

LUCY. I've never been so well—so full of vitality. I was only a poor, washed-out, pale creature. I don't know what made you love me, John. There was no reason why you should. But there is *now.*

HARKER. I worship you.

LUCY. Then tell me something, John. (HARKER *turns slightly away.)* If you love me, you'll tell me. (HARKER *turns front.)* Now don't turn away from me again.

HARKER. *(Wearily and sadly)* You made me promise that I wouldn't tell you—anything.

LUCY. Oh, but I release you from your promise. There, now. What were you and Father and the funny Professor doing all day?

HARKER. I can't tell you. I promised.

LUCY. *(Angrily)* You say you love me, but you don't trust me.

HARKER. I would trust you with my life, my soul.

LUCY. Then prove it. What were you doing— over there in Carfax? With the hammer and the horrible iron stake. *(He shakes his head. She registers anger. He puts his head in his hands, as though crying.)* You don't think I'm asking you because— I'm just trying to find out whether you really love me. (HARKER *recoils from her, facing up.*) So you try to hide your schemes and your plots. Afraid I'd give them away, are you? You fools. Whatever *he* wants to know, he finds out for himself. He knows what you do. He knows what you think. He knows everything.

HARKER. Lucy! (*Puts his head in her lap and sobs.* LUCY *makes clawlike movement with both her hands, then as he sobs she changes attitude and gently strokes his head.*)

LUCY. My dear, I'm sorry. Let me kiss away the tears. (*She starts to kiss him. He quickly rises; backs away a few steps.*)

HARKER. No, you mustn't kiss me. You made me promise not to let you kiss me.

LUCY. You don't know why I said that, John darling. It was because I love you so much. I was afraid of what might happen. You've always thought me cold, but I've blood in my veins, hot blood, my John. And I knew if I were to kiss you— but I'm not afraid now. Come, will you make me say it?

HARKER. (*Backs step away from her*) Lucy, I don't understand you.

LUCY. (*Moves toward him*) I love you. I want you. (*Stretches out her arms to him*) Come to me, my darling. I want you.

HARKER. (*Goes to her, his resistance overcome, carried away by her ardor*) Lucy, Lucy! (*He seizes her in his arms. Slowly she takes his head and bends it back. Slowly, triumphantly she bends her head down, drawing back her upper lips. DOGS howl outside. Her mouth hovers over his. She bends his head further back quickly. Her mouth seeks his throat. Doors c. open.* VAN HELSING *rushes in, holding crucifix in right hand.*)

VAN HELSING. Harker! Harker, save yourself! (HARKER *rises and to* C. *With outstretched arm*

holds crucifix between them. Her face becomes con-
vulsed with loathing and rage. She snarls like an
animal, retreats, fainting onto divan. VAN HEL-
SING *follows, crossing to* R. *end of couch; holds*
crucifix to her; strokes her forehead with left hand)
I warned you, my poor friend. *(He kneels beside*
LUCY; *begins to chafe her temples. She revives*
slowly, looks about her, sees cross and stretches out
arm to it. VAN HELSING *picks cross up. She seizes*
it and kisses it passionately. VAN HELSING, *fervent-*
ly) Thank God! Thank God! *(Pause.* HARKER
crosses end of divan.)

LUCY. *(Broken-hearted)* Don't come to me, John.
I am unclean. *(He sits on divan,* L. *of her.)*

HARKER. My darling, in my eyes you are purity
itself.

VAN HELSING. You love her, and in love there is
truth. She is pure, and the evil thing that has entered her shall be rooted out.

LUCY. *(In weak voice as in previous Acts to* VAN
HELSING*)* You said you could save Mina's soul.

VAN HELSING. Mina's soul is in Heaven. *(*SEW-
ARD *opens door* C.*)*

LUCY. *(Murmurs)* Tell me how. *(Enter* SEW-
ARD C. *to* L. *of divan. He comes up to* GROUP *in alarm,*
but VAN HELSING *motions silence.)*

VAN HELSING. It is your right to know—now. I
entered her tomb. I pried open the coffin. I found
her there, sleeping, but not dead—not truly dead.
There was blood in her cheeks, a drop of blood like
a red ruby on the corner of her mouth. With a
stake and hammer I struck to the heart. One scream,
a convulsion, and then—the look of peace that came
to her face when with God's help I had made her
truly dead. *(During this speech* LUCY *leaves cruci-*
fix at her side on divan.)

LUCY. If I die, swear to me that you will do this
to my body.

VAN HELSING. It shall be done.

HARKER. I swear it.

SEWARD. And I.

LUCY. My lover, my father, my dear friend, you have sworn to save my soul. And now I am done with life. I cannot live on to become—what you know.

VAN HELSING. No, no, Miss Lucy, by all you hold sacred, you must not even think of suicide. That would put you in his power forever.

LUCY. I cannot face this horror that I am becoming.

HARKER. *(Rises)* We will find this *thing* that has fouled your life, destroy him and send his soul to burning hell, and it shall be by my hand.

LUCY. *(Stopping him by gesture)* You must destroy him if you can, but with pity in your hearts, not rage and vengeance. That poor soul who has done so much evil needs our prayers more than any other——

HARKER. No, you cannot ask me to forgive.

LUCY. Perhaps I, too, will need your prayers and your pity.

VAN HELSING. *(Sitting R. of her on divan)* My dear Miss Lucy, now, while you are yourself, help me. *(Takes her hand.)*

LUCY. How can I help you? Don't tell me, no, you mustn't tell me anything.

VAN HELSING. Each time the white face, the red eyes came you were pale, exhausted afterwards. But that last time——

LUCY. *(Shudders)* Last time he came he said I was his bride, he would seal me to him for the centuries to come.

VAN HELSING. And then?

LUCY. And then—— *(Rises; crosses toward C. door)* No, no, I can't tell you. I can't——

VAN HELSING. But you must.

SEWARD. You must, Lucy.

LUCY. He scratched open one of his veins. He pressed my mouth down to it. He called it a mystic sacrament—he made me—he made me drink——— I can't, I can't—go on——— *(Rushes off* C. *hysterically.* SEWARD *follows her off* C. HARKER *crosses to chair* R. *of desk.)*

VAN HELSING. *(Crosses to* L.C.*)* I warned you, my poor friend. I broke in when I heard the dogs howling.

HARKER. The dogs. Then the Werewolf is about.

VAN HELSING. He is pursuing Renfield.

HARKER. *(Rises; crosses down* L.*)* God, we must do something.

VAN HELSING. And at once. I shall leave Renfield here, as I did Miss Lucy. If the *thing* appears, we three will bar the two doors and the window.

HARKER. *(Crosses up toward window. Laughs bitterly)* Bar? Against *that?*

VAN HELSING. Even against *that,* for we shall each carry the sacred element.

HARKER. *(Crosses* L. *of desk)* And then?

VAN HELSING. Then I do not know. It will be terrible, for we do not know his full powers. But this I know——— *(Looks at watch)* It is eight minutes to sunrise. The power of all evil things ceases with the coming of day. His one last earth box is his only refuge. If we can keep him here till daybreak he must collapse. And the stake and the hammer are ready. *(DOGS howl. HARKER crosses to window.)* He is here. Come quickly. (VAN HELSING *runs to window. Seizes* RENFIELD.*)*

RENFIELD. *(As he is dragged in by* VAN HELSING*)* No, no!

VAN HELSING. But you must, man, and this may save your soul and your life as well.

RENFIELD. No, no, no, not alone. Don't leave me alone. (VAN HELSING *shoves him forward.* REN-

FIELD *falls.* VAN HELSING *hurries out, closing door*
C., *putting LIGHTS OUT.* RENFIELD *slowly rises;*
looks about him. RENFIELD *howls in terror; crouches*
in firelight as far away as possible from doors and
window. Retreats to footlights R. DRACULA *appears,*
door C., *in PALE BLUE LIGHT, in evening*
clothes, dress and cloak as before. RED LIGHT
from fireplace covers DRACULA. *As* DRACULA *moves,*
RENFIELD'S *back is to audience.)* Master. I didn't
do it. I said nothing. I am your slave, your dog.
(DRACULA *steps toward him.)* Master, don't kill me.
For the love of God, let me live. Punish me—torture me—I deserve it—but let me live. I can't face
God with all those lives on my conscience, all that
blood on my hands.

DRACULA. *(With deadly calm)* Did I not promise you that you should come to me at your death,
and enjoy centuries of life and power over the bodies
and souls of others?

RENFIELD. Yes, Master, I want lives, I want blood
—but I didn't want human life.

DRACULA. You betrayed me. You sought to warn
my destined bride against me.

RENFIELD. Mercy, mercy, mercy, don't kill me!

(DRACULA *raises right arm very slowly toward* REN-
FIELD, *who screams, this time in physical pain.*
RENFIELD, *like a bird before a snake, drags him-*
self to DRACULA, *who stands motionless. As*
RENFIELD *reaches* DRACULA'S *feet,* DRACULA,
with swift motion, stoops, seizes him by the
throat, lifts him up, his grip stifling RENFIELD'S
screams. Doors C. *thrown open.* VAN HELSING
switches on LIGHTS. DRACULA *drops* REN-
FIELD, *who falls into corner below couch and re-*
mains there during following scene. DRACULA
starts toward VAN HELSING, *who takes case*
containing Host out of inside breast pocket and

holds it out toward DRACULA *in his clenched right fist.* DRACULA *recoils; turns quickly to window.* HARKER *appears through window and holds crucifix toward* DRACULA *in clenched fist.* DRACULA *recoils and turns to down* R. SEWARD *enters window, holding crucifix when* HARKER *does. The* THREE MEN *stand during the following scene with right arms pointing toward* DRACULA. *He turns, walks to fireplace, turns and faces them.)*

DRACULA. *(R., back to audience—ironically)* My friends, I regret I was not present to receive your calls at my house.

VAN HELSING. *(Looks at watch)* Four minutes until sunrise.

DRACULA. *(Crossing to below sofa, looking at wrist watch)* Your watch is correct, Professor. *(Facing down* R.)

VAN HELSING. *(Step* C.) Your life in death has reached its end.

SEWARD. *(Step toward* C.) By God's mercy.

DRACULA. (HARKER *steps toward* DRACULA. DRACULA, *turning to them, suavely)* It's end? Not yet, Professor. I have still more than three minutes to add to my five hundred years.

HARKER. And three minutes from now you'll be in hell, where a thousand years of agony will not bring you one second nearer the end of your punishment.

VAN HELSING. Silence, Harker. Miss Lucy forbade this. She asked for prayer, and for pity. *(To* DRACULA*)* Make your peace with God, Man-That-Was. We are not your judges—we know not how this curse may have come upon you.

DRACULA. *(Furiously)* You fools! You think with your wafers, your wolf's-bane, you can destroy me. me, the king of my kind? You shall see. Five

of my earth boxes you have polluted. Have you
found the sixth?

VAN HELSING. You cannot reach your sixth
refuge now. Take your true form as Werewolf if
you will. Your fangs may rend us, but we have each
sworn to keep you here—*(Looks at watch)* —for
two minutes and a half, when you must collapse and
we can make an end.

DRACULA. *(Crosses to L. of couch)* You keep *me.*
Fools, listen and let my words ring in your ears all
your lives, and torture you on your deathbeds. I go,
I go to sleep in my box for a hundred years. You
have accomplished that much against me, Van Helsing. But in a century I shall wake, and call my
bride to my side from her tomb, my Lucy, my
Queen. *(On line "My Lucy, my Queen," HARKER
and SEWARD step in.)* I have other brides of old
times who await me in their vaults in Transylvania.
But I shall set her above them all.

HARKER. Should you escape, we know how to save
Lucy's soul, if not her life.

DRACULA. *(Stepping in to L. of divan)* Ah, the
stake. Yes, but only if she dies by day. I shall see
that she dies by night. She shall come to an earth
box of mine at her death and await her Master. To
do to her what you did to my Mina, Van Helsing,
you must find her body, and that you will not.

HARKER. Then she shall die by day.

DRACULA. *(Crosses to C.)* You will kill her? You
lack the courage, you poor rat of flesh and blood.

SEWARD. Silence, John—he is doomed. This is
his revenge. He hopes to trouble us—afterwards.

VAN HELSING. *(Looks at watch)* Thirty seconds.
(They move in.)

DRACULA. *(Calmly, suavely again)* I thank you
for reminding me of the time.

VAN HELSING. Harker, open the curtains. (HAR-
KER *opens curtains. RED LIGHT of approaching*

dawn outside.) That is the East. The sun will rise beyond the meadow there. (DRACULA *pulls cape over his head.)*

SEWARD. *(Glancing behind, leaves wolf's-bane on desk as he looks up at window)* The clouds are coloring.

HARKER. God's daybreak. (HARKER *leaves crucifix on desk.* VAN HELSING *watches watch.* SEWARD *and* HARKER *step in.)*

DRACULA. *(Coolly. Turns upstage, with back to them, and if trap is used, gets to position on trap)* A pleasant task you have set yourself, Mr. Harker.

VAN HELSING. Ten seconds. Be ready when he collapses. (SEWARD *crosses to hold* DRACULA'S *cape on* L. *of* DRACULA. HARKER *holds cape on* R. *of* DRACULA.)

HARKER. The sun! The stake, Professor—the stake! Hold him, Doctor.

SEWARD. I've got him.

(DRACULA, *with loud burst of mocking laughing, goes down trap on the word "sun," leaving the* TWO MEN *holding the empty cape. As soon as they've seen trap back in place,* HARKER *backs down* L., *drops empty cape in front of desk, then a FLASH goes off in front of fireplace. If the trap is not used, the flash goes on the word "Sun," then a complete BLACKOUT. LIGHTS come on as soon as* DRACULA *is off stage through* C. *door.* HARKER *and* SEWARD *are holding cape, then business is the same. The* THREE MEN *look around them.)*

                (WARN Curtain and BLACKOUT.)

HARKER. Up the chimney, as a bat. You heard what he said?

SEWARD. *(Crosses down to* HARKER*)* God will not permit it. What's to be done now, Van Helsing?

VAN HELSING. *(Crosses down* R.C., *after looking at the prostrate* RENFIELD; *motions* HARKER *and* SEWARD *to him. Whispers to them before and speaks)* We'll trick Renfield into showing us.

(If the disappearing trap and cloak are not used, ad lib. the line following the blackout at this point, PROFSSOR *saying, "Who the devil put out the lights?" Very noisy, dramatic ad lib. through here.)*

VAN HELSING. Dare we leave Renfield on earth to become the slave when he dies?

SEWARD. But he's human. We can't do murder?

HARKER. I'll do it if you won't, Doctor!

VAN HELSING. *(To* SEWARD*)* Go to your office and get some painless drug.

RENFIELD. *(Sensing their drift without hearing their words, has been edging toward panel. Looks around room, then at panel)* They're going to kill me, Master. Save me. I am coming to you. *(Panel* R.C. *opens,* RENFIELD *exits and panel closes. They rush to panel.)*

VAN HELSING. He has shown us the way. Where does that passage go?

SEWARD. I never knew there was a passage. *(*HARKER *to desk; gets stake and hammer from desk. They rush to panel.)*

VAN HELSING. Only that devil has the combination. We'll break through somehow. Harker—quick, the hammer.

BLACK OUT

CURTAIN

ACT THREE

SCENE II

SCENE: *Played in a black cyclorama. Absolute DARKNESS. Coffin* R.C. *and back of gauze drop. FLASH of electric torch seen coming slowly downstairs* C. *Coffin contains dummy body of* DRACULA.

VAN HELSING'S VOICE. For God's sake, be careful, Seward.

SEWARD'S VOICE. These stairs go down forever.

VAN HELSING'S VOICE. May God protect us.

SEWARD'S VOICE. Is Harker there?

VAN HELSING'S VOICE. He's gone for a lantern.

SEWARD'S VOICE. I've got to the bottom.

VAN HELSING'S VOICE. Be careful. I'm right behind you. *(TORCH FLASHES around stage and they walk about slowly.)*

SEWARD'S VOICE. What can this place be?

VAN HELSING'S VOICE. It seems an old vault. *(Stifled scream from* SEWARD. *TORCH OUT. The torch is seen to jerk back.)* What is it? Oh, where are you, man?

SEWARD'S VOICE. Sorry. I'm all right. A big rat ran across my foot. *(LIGHT seen coming downstairs.* HARKER *appears carrying lighted lantern which reaches floor; partially illuminates bare vault. He has stake and hammer in left hand.)*

HARKER. Where are you? What is this place?

VAN HELSING. We can't see. *(HARKER moves with lantern.)*

72

HARKER. The place smells horribly of bats.

VAN HELSING. It has an animal smell, like the lair of a wolf.

HARKER. That's what it is.

SEWARD. *(Still flashing torch about)* There's absolutely nothing here.

HARKER. *(At extreme L. with lantern)* Here's another passage.

VAN HELSING. *(Moving L.)* I thought so. That must lead to Carfax. The sixth earth box is hidden somewhere here.

HARKER. And the monster is in it.

SEWARD. You can't be sure. *(As he speaks light from his torch falls on* RENFIELD, *stretched on floor, down* R. RENFIELD *screams as light falls on him; scurries off* R. *into darkness.)* Renfield. (HARKER *and* VAN HELSING *hurry across.)*

VAN HELSING. Where is he?

SEWARD. Over there somewhere. Even if Renfield knew about this place, that doesn't prove the vampire's here.

VAN HELSING. *(As* SEWARD *is speaking* VAN HELSING *moves* R.; *seizes* RENFIELD*)* It is the vampire's life or yours. *(Drags* RENFIELD *into light of lantern)* Look at him, man, look at him. He knows.

RENFIELD. I know nothing. Let me go. Let me go, I say. *(Breaks away; goes* R.*)*

VAN HELSING. He was stretched here, but he wouldn't let me drag him back. Ah! Here it is. Quick, that stake. (HARKER *and* VAN HELSING, *with stake, pry up stone slab and open coffin. The* THREE MEN *gaze in horror and triumph at coffin.)*

SEWARD. What a horrible undead thing he is lying there.   *(WARN Curtain)*

HARKER. Let me drive it in deep!

(VAN HELSING, *kneeling facing audience, takes*

stake from HARKER, *places it carefully in hole.*
RENFIELD *at* R. *end of coffin.)*

VAN HELSING. *(Almost in a whisper)* That's over
the heart, Doctor?

SEWARD. *(Back of coffin)* Yes. (VAN HELSING
hands hammer to HARKER. HARKER *raises hammer
high over head; strikes with full force. Low GROAN
backstage* C. *Silence. Stake remains fixed in* DRAC-
ULA'S *body, the top of stake visible to audience.)*

VAN HELSING. See his face now—the look of
peace. (HARKER *pulls string that pulls cape over*
DRACULA'S *face.)*

SEWARD. He is crumbling away.

RENFIELD. Thank God, we're free!

LUCY. *(Comes down stairway and halts at bottom)* Father, Father, John!

HARKER. Lucy!

VAN HELSING. *(Takes handful of dust; scatters
it over the body)* Dust to dust—ashes to ashes.

CURTAIN

(When Curtain hits floor—the gauze goes up—
ENTIRE CAST *comes down stage and Black Drop
comes down in one for curtain speech. Curtain
rises.)*   *(WARN Curtain.)*

VAN HELSING. *(To* AUDIENCE*)* Just a moment,
Ladies and Gentlemen! Just a word before you go.
We hope the memories of Dracula and Renfield
won't give you bad dreams, so just a word of reas-
surance. When you get home tonight and the lights
have been turned out and you are afraid to look
behind the curtains and you dread to see a face appear at the window—why, just pull yourself together and remember that after all *there are such
things. (Curtain falls.)*

END OF PLAY

"DRACULA"

ELECTRICAL PLOT

Electrical Equipment necessary:

1 Switchboard with facilities for handling 9 baby
 spots, one 1000 watt bunch, three 1000 watt
 spots, all on separate dimmers, and two sections
 of Hercules borders on dimmers.
2 Sections Hercules borders, lamps in same to be
 alternately amber and straw.
2—1000 watt bunch lights.
6—1000 watt spots.
9—250 watt baby spots.
2—3 light brackets.
2—1 light brackets.
1 table lamp.
1 flash box.
1—2 light strip (masked in so does not spread).
1—firelog.
1 smoke effect (for mist in Act II).
2—6-way plugging boxes, cable, etc.

Lighting Equipment in First Border for Entire Play:
 (see diagram)

5 *Baby spots* on left of pipe, as follows:
 No. 1 green covers right stage.
 No. 2 amber covers right end of couch in Act II,
 also table up L.

No. 3 amber covers c. door in Acts I and III.
No. 4 green covers door up L. in Act II.
No. 5 green covers chair back of desk, Act III.

1 Section 6 lamp Hercules covers Left side of stage.

1 Section 6 lamp Hercules covers Right side of stage.

(Hercules border focussed so there is practically no
light on back wall.)
2 Baby Spots in center of pipe between the two sections of Hercules as follows:
No. 6 green covers French window up L. in Act
III.
No. 7 amber covers couch R. in Acts I and III.
1 Baby Spot extreme R. end of pipe:
No. 8 Green covers couch up L.C. and R.C. of stage
in Act II.

2—1000 Watt Flood Lights from front hang in
front of first balcony, one green—one blue.

ACT ONE

2—3-Light brackets above fireplace.
1 Table lamp on up-stage end of desk Left.
2—1000 Watt blue bunch lights at opposite ends and
focussed on exterior backing L.
1—1000 Watt blue moonlight spot focussed in window L.
1—Red Spot coming from fireplace R., focussed on
Right half of couch R.
1—25 Watt lamp outside and above door up C.

At Rise:

Foots out except 2-light amber strip in front of
couch R.

Hercules border up ¾.
2 Wall Brackets on.
Table Lamp on.
2 Blue 1000 Watt Bunches on exterior backing
    up L.
1 Blue 1000 Watt Spot coming in window up L.
1 Red Baby Spot coming from fireplace focussed on
    R. half of couch R.
Small lamp in firelogs.
1—25 Watt Lamp outside and above door up C.

No. 7 Spot on Couch
    On Cue, "Do you think this new man will be any
        better?"
No. 3 Spot on Door
    On Cue, "Count Dracula."
No. 3 Spot Dims Out
    When Dracula goes down stage.
No. 7 Spot Dims Out
    When Lucy leaves couch.
No. 3 Spot On Door
    On Cue, "You wish to consult the anxious father."
No. 3 Spot Dims Out
    After Dracula exits.
Lights Out except Fireplace and Moonlight, when
    Van Helsing presses switch.
Fireplace and Moonlight Out
    When Lucy screams.
Lights On
    When Van Helsing presses switch.

ACT TWO

1—1-Light bracket on wall R. between door R.1 and
    French Window R.
1—1-Light bracket on wall L. between door and arch
    and upstage of mirror.

1—Blue 1000 Watt Bunch covering exterior back-
    ing R. and from R.
2—1000 Watt Blue Spots from pipe upstage cover-
    ing space outside window.
1—Green Baby Spot on floor back of scrim tapestry
    upstage R.C.

At Rise:

Foots out.
Hercules border up ¾.
2 Wall Brackets on.
No. 2 Amber Spot on, covering Left end of couch
    and table at R. of arch up L.
1—Blue 1000 Watt Bunch covering exterior back-
    ing up R.
2—1000 Watt Blue Spots on pipe hanging above
    window R. and covering space outside window.
1 Smoke effect outside window.

All Lights Out
    When Maid crosses L. after scene with Dr. Seward.
No. 1 Green Spot on (Covering R. stage)
    Count of 6 after black out.
No. 1 Green Spot Dim Out
    On Cue, "Will reach you soon."
Lights On
    Count of 4 after Green Spot out.
Green Spot Back of Scrim Tapestry On.
    When Maid places hands to forehead.
Smoke Effect (for mist)
    When Maid opens French window.
All Lights Out
    When Maid exits R.1.
No. 4 Green Spot On. (Covering door up L.)
    Count of 5 after black out.
No. 8 Green Spot On
    When Dracula crosses R.

No. 4 Green Spot Dims Out
  When No. 8. Green comes on.
Green Flood From Front
  Comes on at the same time as No. 8 Spot.

ACT THREE

(Same as Act One)

Scene I.

Flash Box in front of fireplace.

At Rise:

  Same as Act I except Red Baby Spot from the
  fireplace focussed on window up L. and the 1000
  Watt Lamp at R. end of exterior backing is
  changed to red and is out at rise.

No. 6 Green Spot On
  As soon as Curtain is well up.
No. 6 Green Spot Dim Out
  Immediately after curtains flap on the French
  window.
No. 5 Green Spot (Covering chair back of desk)
  Comes on as No. 6 Green Spot dims out.
No. 5 Green Spot Dim Out
  After chair back of desk moves.
No. 6 Green Spot On
  As soon as No. 5 Green Spot dims out.
No. 6 Green Spot Dims Out
  After curtains flap on French window.
No. 7 Amber Spot (Covering couch R.)
  On Cue, "You mustn't mind that poor crazed
  creature."
No. 7 Spot Off
  On Cue, "I can't tell you. I can't tell you."

Blue Foots Up ¼ (Sneak them in)
  When Lucy exits.
Lights Out, except Moonlight, blue foots and fire-
    place
  When Van Helsing presses switch.
Lights On and Blue Foots Out
  When Van Helsing presses switch.
Red 1000 Watt Bunch (Covering exterior backing)
  Bring up slowly to ¼ on cue, "I shall set her above
    them all."
Flash (in front of fireplace)
  When Harker drops Dracula's cape to floor.
All Lights Out
  On Cue, "Quick, Harker, the hammer."

No House Lights between Scenes I and II.
Blue Foots up ¼.

ACT III—SCENE II

Lantern for Harker.
Flashlight for Seward.
Small green 25 watt lamp in coffin, covering face
    of dummy only.
At Rise:
  All lights out.
Blue Flood From Front.
  On cue, "Look at him, man. He knows."
No. 1 Green Spot (Covering coffin R.)
  On cue, "He was stretched here."

As soon as Act curtain down, throw in white foots,
    full up, for Curtain speech.

"DRACULA"

PROPERTY PLOT

ACT I

1—Ground Cloth 36 feet by 21 feet.
2—Fire Dogs.
1—Center rug—9 x 12.
1—Fireplace with Mantel, R.2.
Five scatter rugs.
1—Overstuff Armchair down R. stage—dark shade, preferably green.
1—Large Davenport—dark brown.
1—Small Stand back of Davenport.
1—Fancy Pillow on Davenport—dark material.
1 Box for cigarettes for Mantel.
1—Smoking Stand with matches.
1 Vase for Mantel with flowers.
1—Trick bookcase, one half of which slides, other half swings.
2—Chairs, one for each side of bookcase.
1—Bellcord of flat tapestry material, to hang on thickness (Pilaster) up Center.
I—Trick armchair for back of desk down L.—see blueprint.
1—Flat-top desk.
1 small cane-seat chair R. of desk.
Piece of tapestry on desk.
2—book ends and books for desk.
1—Blotting pad.

10—open letters in letter file.

1—paper knife.

1—ink stand.

1—tray for pencils, pen, etc.

1—glass ashtray with matches.

1—small blotting pad.

5—or 6 medical report forms.

Plenty of typewriter paper.

1—pad of note paper.

2—curtains and valance on arch to work (practical).

1—set of curtains same material for double doors
   with valance—not practical.

3—lamp chimneys each side of stage for actors to
   bark into for dog barks.
   (Practice with these chimneys, using top for
   mouthpiece, by holding hand over end farther
   away from mouth and using hand as trombonist
   uses stiff hat in orchestra, a weird barking effect
   can be accomplished. This is one of the most
   effective tricks in the play if done correctly.)

2—siren whistles to blow with mouth for bat effect.

1—black bat to work on fish line (8 foot pole).

Same bat to work on fish line at cue. This bat flies
   into set. For directions how to work this bat,
   see directions accompanying.

50—feet of 50-pound black fishline for bat effect
   (flying bat).

1—Physician's bag containing magnifying glass,
   sprig of Wolf's-bane (dried laurel).

Green book off stage R. for Dracula. Uses at final
   speech of Act.

Megaphone for Renfield off stage.

ACT II

1—center rug—9 x 12.

5—small rugs, same as Act I.

1—iron day bed with mattress—green cover to match curtains, 3 green pillows.

1—small dressing table Left of arch with 3 small books, small smelling-salt bottle.

1—Small stand R. of arch up Left, with small vase with one or two rosebuds. (This is the vase Dracula throws to break "mirror.")

1—small ashtray with small sponge for this table to be used for blood effect.

1—console table above door L.1.

1—Bronze Statue on table.

1—Iron frame 14" x 24" hang above console for mirror effect. (See blueprint.)

1—Box to hang off stage side of mirror to catch broken glass. (See blueprint.)

1—English newspaper, folded once. (London "Times.")

For Van Helsing:

1—Continental Telegram.

1—Cardboard box containing wolf's-bane (dried laurel), necklace.

2—Sprigs of wolf's-bane inside box.

1—Rosary and beads. This should be lengthened with extra beads large enough to be slipped over and off Lucy's head at cues. The ordinary rosary is not large *enough for this business.*

1—handkerchief.

1—small penknife.

1—black Host made of velvet—see blueprint.

1—six-foot ladder, to work bat on pole.

1—Pole.

1—Armchair down R.1.

2—Revolvers for stage manager—in good condition to shoot blanks.

1—one small music stand for fish reel for bat line so line will not become foul when not in use.

1—set black draw curtains for Vision Scene.
1—piece tapestry for wall over couch.

ACT III—SCENE I

Furniture same as Act I.
    Small table back of davenport (divan) may be struck to facilitate quick change.
Large sledge hammer and iron stake, about 18" long, on upper end of desk.
1—trick armchair—the trick part is used in this act. (See blueprint.)
1—crank for under stage to be used on this chair. (See blueprint.)
For Van Helsing—cross and crucifix, not over 7 inches long.
For Harker—cross and crucifix, not over 7 inches long.
For Dr. Seward—Cross and crucifix, not over 7 inches long.
1—prop. black cloak with cape for Dracula.

ACT III—SCENE II

1 Tomb (coffin) with Dummy body in evening dress.
1—cigar box of sand for Van Helsing in side of Tomb. (Box filled with sand and sawdust for stake downstage side of dummy.)
1—small vest pocket flashlight for Dr. Seward.
1—Lantern, very dim, for Harker.
    Same hammer and stake as is used in First Scene—Act III.
1—megaphone for Dracula—offstage for groan at his death.

Play this Scene behind a scrim gauze drop. This drop we light from 2 blue spots thrown from

balcony—but these lights are not absolutely necessary.

Also use black draw-curtains same as a musical-show close in, which when tied off make the teaser. When in use we drop this draw at the same time the house curtain comes down, take up scrim, the actors swiftly come through the split in the draw curtains so as to be in position when house Curtain rises for the bow and the Curtain speech.

This Curtain speech is one of the most effective pieces of the play. The quicker the actors are in position before the audience files out, the better, for it enables Van Helsing to stop them with his:

"One moment, Ladies and Gentlemen," etc.

"DRACULA"

NOTES ON PRODUCTION

ACT I

Should be painted a very *deep* tone of *dark* brown, in order that, when lighted, the walls will lend an atmosphere of mystery. Trim your X-rays or Hercules on the pipe back of Concert border so they will not shine or reflect on the back wall. This is extremely necessary, as practically all the situations in the play are staged so that they are no further upstage than ten feet from the curtain line. This, provided, of course, that the set is fourteen feet deep from the curtain line to the pilaster (thickness) in the Center of the back flat. It will be found efficacious to use a small yellow spot irised down to almost a pin spot focussed from the pipe (see electric diagram on blueprint) to the double doors upstage Center for the entrances and exits of Dracula —Act I and Act III, Scene I.

On the blueprint of Act I, a spot (red medium) is thrown from a very short offstage stand through the fireplace, its rays shining just over the upstage R. end of the divan. Care should be exercised in focussing this spot with its red medium on this particular end of the divan, which is downstage R., as this is where Dracula's "ghostly" hand appears after all lights, but the fireplace spot, have been blacked-out by Van Helsing near the end of Act I. Dracula makes his entrance for this situation through the L.

side of the trick bookcase, crawls on his hands and knees to back (upstage) end of the divan where first his hand appears over the head of Lucy, and then the top of his head begins to be visible to the audience, at which point she screams and all lights blackout. Dracula makes his escape during the blackout, through the swinging door (left half of bookcase), removes the black fencing vest which he has worn over his white dress shirt for this situation, gets into this dress coat again, and enters (arch double doors) at cue for his lines at curtain—"The patient is better, I hope?"

The Bookcase is made so that one-half stage R. end—slides off stage, while the L. side is on spring hinges and swings offstage. A small bolt at top on the inside of the bookcase door that swings offstage will assist in keeping this door closed except when in use. It is better to have Dracula manipulate this bolt than for a stagehand to handle it. The sliding part of the bookcase, however, *should be* manipulated by a stagehand. This sliding part of the bookcase should be in a groove treated with mica in order to eliminate any noise. This part of the bookcase is not used until the Third Act when it is opened for Renfield to make his escape at the cue, "Master, Master, I am coming to you."

On the pilaster (thickness) upstage c. is an oldfashioned tapestry material bell-pull. Back of the divan is a very small table, not over a foot in diameter or a foot square on the top, where Van Helsing places his small medicine bag in Act I. This can be struck in Act III. The smallness of this table will give more room back of the divan for Dracula when he crawls in at the end of Act I, and will also give more room to Van Helsing in Act I when he searches in the bag to find the wolf's-bane and takes position up back of the L. end of the divan just be-

fore he pushes the wolf's-bane under Renfield's
nose. The chair downstage R., against the R. flat,
and between the fireplace and the curtain, should
be a rather large low armchair.

Regarding the desk, L.C., would suggest that this
be not too enormous as there are several pieces of
business about it, like the circling of Dracula at the
end of the First Act in order for him to get around
to a position by the window and up by the door as
Lucy is being assisted off stage through the double
doors.

The small chair at the upstage end of this desk
should be, if possible, about the size of a telephone
chair used in residences, only with the seat as low
as an ordinary chair. Van Helsing handles this chair
several times and its smallness and lightness facili-
tates this handling. For the trick chair, back of the
desk, use a rather large armchair, with legs strong
enough so that it may be turned, with an auger-
shaped iron from beneath stage, at the cue in Act III.
The two chairs upstage against the back wall in
Act I can be of any design or period that will lend
dignity and perhaps mystery to the room.

The curtains on the double doors upstage C.
should be made of some very dark green or brown
material to add to the mystery of the scene. These
curtains and a valance are not practical. The curtains and valance on the arch L.C. (Act II) *should
be practical* and of the same material as that used
for the doors. The practical curtains are used with
several pieces of business during Act I and the
First Scene of Act III. These curtains should be
controlled by a sliding cord working from the upstage end.

It is absolutely necessary to have a black canopy-
topped backing back of the bookcase offstage, so that
any stray light backstage doesn't hit Dracula mak-

ing his exit and entrance to frighten Lucy while the
stage is in the blackout in Act I, and Renfield's escape in Act III, Scene I.

THE FLYING BAT

The bat effect should be as carefully rehearsed
as the play itself. This bat can be made of a strip
of wood about 10″ to 12″ long and 2½″ to 3″ wide
and about ½″ to ⅞″ thick. A wire coat-hanger can
be nailed to this piece of wood for the wings, and
the whole framework covered with some kind of
black cloth, either black canton flannel or black mus-
lin—not glazed. A screw-eye should be inserted in
the back of the bat at a point where it balances, when
connected by a fishline swivel which, in turn, is connected with the fishline itself. There are two pieces
of this fifty-pound black fishline to be used. One
controls the back of the bat and the other the tail.
The fishline that is tied to the swivel in the back of
the bat should be started from a point downstage
outside the door in Act I, and controlled by a property man. This line, which he holds in his hand, is
drawn up over the ceiling flat and enters the set
through a hole bored in the center batten of the ceiling. When not in use, and during changes of sets,
the onstage end should be tied off with a fishline
dipsy, and when in use this dipsy is removed. When
the bat is not in use, but ready for work in Act I,
it is drawn off by the line attached to the tail through
the windows L.—the line from downstage L. being
of sufficient length to allow this. The flying bat line
is tied off in such a way that the opening and closing of the curtains do not foul it, nor does it foul
them.

The method of operating the bat effect is as follows: After the property man outside the window
has tied the line to the tail of the bat, he holds this

line in his left hand so that it can run through his fingers swiftly. At the cue, he throws the bat into the room through the window. At this cue, the property man down stage L. back of offstage tormentor begins to pull swiftly on his line and he pulls the bat so swiftly its momentum carries it beyond the hole Center in the ceiling. Use a grummet or smooth solid screw eye so that line will not foul. At this point the man outside the window begins to haul in on his line—the man downstage paying out enough line so as to keep the bat from falling too close to the floor, but giving it a sense of reality— until the bat is back in his hands outside the window. Don't be alarmed if this bat, on its way out, strikes the sides of the windows, as this will heighten rather than destroy the effect. Properly rehearsed, this "flying" bat will cause a startling effect on the audience.

There is another bat effect, but this second bat does not fly on the cord. It is used in the Renfield scene in Act I. The purpose of the swivel on the bat (if only one bat is used) is so that the bat itself can be unhooked from the fishline which makes its fly and used when tied to either a fishpole or a stage brace if the latter is not too heavy to manipulate. In preparation for the cue, a property man stands on a ladder and swings this bat in the window as though he were casting for a fish.

In Act I the swinging bat works once and the flying bat once. In Act II the flying bat works once and the swinging bat works once. In this Second Act, however, the bat works through the French windows up R.

CLOTHES WORN IN ACT ONE

As to the clothes worn in Act I, Dracula wears full evening dress. If he uses a deep green makeup, lining with red highlighted by rubbing off the green and allowing some parts of the flesh to show through, the makeup gives a weird and eerie effect, and causes shudders on the part of the audience when Dracula makes his first entrance. Incidentally, Dracula should have and use a deep, heavy voice, but he should not play his part too heavily. Even in the First Scene of the Third Act, when Dracula is trapped in the room by Van Helsing and his associates, while Dracula, of course, waxes melodramatic, he shouldn't overplay the part.

Lucy should wear a long negligee that is semi-revealing. Lucy is supposed to be anæmic, but she should use volume enough so that there will not be a singsong in her voice nor produce an effect of pity. She should gain sympathy, but not pity. The success of her first scene in Act I will depend on how she is able to picture to the audience the dream she has had, while telling it to Van Helsing.

Van Helsing should wear either a dark Oxford suit of some material that doesn't conflict with any other members of the cast. He should use either powder or silver aluminum on his hair. He wears the same suit throughout the play.

John Harker, in Act I, may wear plus-fours of gray material.

Seward wears a tuxedo in Act I. Upon him depends the tempo of the piece. The thought in his mind at all times, when speaking to Van Helsing, is, "What about my daughter? My daughter is dying!" In the scene where Van Helsing describes vampires, the Professor should be, of course, deadly serious, as he is more or less throughout the play, but not to the point of heroic melodrama.

Harker should be anxious to help, of course, but not incredulous. While Seward doesn't at any time during Act I believe that such things as vampires exist, he should be very careful not to make too many movements or overplay the scene while he is seated on the divan when Van Helsing is describing vampires. Much of the success of the play depends on how this scene gets over. If the actors can make the audience believe that there are such supernatural things as vampires, then the rest of the play can be very easily projected across the footlights.

Seward doesn't believe in any of the facts presented by Van Helsing until the Second Act, because as he says in the text—"I was incredulous until I saw that creature hovering over Lucy."

A Red Cross nurse can be used in the lobby. This "stunt" is good publicity, as it sets the mood of the audience as they are being seated. They expect to be thrilled. Unless your audiences are more hardened than the audiences played to in New York and on the road, you will have people fainting in the auditorium for the nurse to take care of, and this is always good for press material.

When the production was staged for Mr. Robert McLaughlin, in Cleveland, we had a very beautiful nurse, dressed in white, who presided over a little alcove in which there was a hospital cot and first-aid appliances. This little "stunt" brought several stories in the newspapers and usually brings comment in the reviews by the critics. Incidentally, as a publicity "stunt" in Cleveland, Mr. McLaughlin used a "Faint Check," somewhat on the order of a baseball rain check. These checks enabled the holder, after an examination by a physician and nurse and countersigned by either one, to return and see a later performance in case they fainted on the night they first attended.

ACT II

The color of the scene should be a very deep green, which, as in the First Act, will lend mystery to the shadowy corners of the room. The Olivette used outside the French windows should have a deep tone blue, and should be turned up toward and light the cyclorama or backing, whichever you use. As quite a few entrances, exits and stage business take place outside this French window, this Olivette should be kept out of the way as much as possible.

The swinging bat and the flying bat work outside this window. Of course a step-ladder must be used for the swinging bat. Dracula makes his first and second entrance through this window. The Attendant and the Maid work up near it. Dr. Seward and Harker go out on the supposed balcony during the scene with Renfield. The spot focussed from the concert border and thrown on the divan (upstage) should be raised enough to cover Lucy when she sits there during the reading of the newspaper, and should be high enough to cover the little stand to the L. of the couch on which there is quite a lot of business. However, this spot should be focussed so that not too much of it shines on the flat back of couch.

It is much better not to use footlights in this Act. In fact, don't use footlights in any of the Acts, with the exception perhaps of the Third Act, and in that Act use them as dim as the dimmers will carry, as they have a bad tendency to reflect on the back wall or else throw too many shadows. Use a dim baby spot (amber) in the footlights, focussed on the stage, L. end of the couch, when Lucy and the Professor play the scene of the examination of the throat, etc.

On the doors of the French windows should be a flat latch and hook. This latch should be made of metal so that it makes a metallic sound when locked by Van Helsing and unlocked by the Maid. When the latter opens the windows at the end of Act II, the steam or vapor effect comes in through these windows and is supposed to resemble fog. When this effect is worked right there is a buzz throughout the entire audience. The vapor can be blown in by a newspaper or fan held in the hand of the man who is working the hose. Any electrical house can supply this vapor effect, which is simply three bottles—one of muriatic acid, one of rose-water and one of ammonia, connected by hose pipes.

There should be a black canopy-topped backing upstage C., back of vision gauze. (First Act bookcase backing may be used.) The onstage side of the gauze is painted to represent tapestry and is lighted at cue by a single green spot, masked by the 2' high base at the bottom. At the cue, Dracula stands in his place, the black draw curtains are opened, the spot is thrown up from the floor to his face, and then the curtains are closed at a given cue. Care should be taken that Dracula doesn't move during this situation, as his white waistcoat and shirtfront may show through the gauze and disturb the scene between the Maid and Lucy if not watched closely. Dracula could very easily light up his own features with a green flashlight held in his hand, instead of the floor spot of green.

Care should be taken that the L. wall of this set is not raked too much.

For the mirror, window-glass is used in the frame that is hung on the flat upstage L. near the arch. On the other side of this flat, to mask the opening of the mirror, a black box is hung on the back of the wing. This box is lined with black Canton flannel, and is used to catch the glass and also the glass flower-holder that Dracula throws when he smashes this mirror at the cue. If this mirror is turned on a rake too much toward the audience, a reflection can be seen by the audience, and this destroys the effect when Van Helsing says to Dracula, "It's reflection covers the whole room, but I cannot see you." The glass flower-holder should be about 10" high and can be purchased at any Five-and-Ten-Cent store. Its base should not be over 2½" in diameter. A small rosebud or two is placed in this vase, so it will not look too obviously a property. This little table on which the vase stands is upstage to the R. of the stage L. end of divan in the embrasure of the 10" jog. On the top of this table it will be to the advantage of Van Helsing if on the top a small cold-cream top of tin is inverted and counter-sunk in the table to hold the sponge containing the red liquid to resemble blood for Van Helsing when he cuts his finger. There is another small table for Van Helsing to use under the mirror where he places the box containing the wolf's-bane and the necklace with the crucifix which is put around Lucy's neck at the end of the Act. The small box should be of cardboard and about 6" square, with folding cover.

The green spot for the hypnotic scene with Dracula and Maid, used in this Act, thrown from the concert border up L. to down R., should strike at a point about the stage L. end of the couch, with sufficient "throw" to also light coffin in Act III, Scene II.

Another green spot, on a dimmer, should cover the arch upstage L. for Dracula's appearance at the end of Act II. Another green spot from the concert border upstage R. should be used for the scene where Dracula bites Lucy.

The dog howls should be done by the members of the cast offstage at the time. The best effect is obtained by barking through an old-fashioned glass lamp chimney. A little practice will give the hollow effect of distance.

I would suggest using a real white mouse in the scene between the Maid and the Attendant. This mouse the Attendant usually takes from his cage and places in a small perforated box which he carries in the pocket of his uniform. At the cue he pulls the box out, gets the mouse by the tail, holds it up to scare Wells, then puts it on his arm, where it runs up sometimes onto his head. This is a great effect, and should be helped out by the emotional fear of the Maid as she is standing on the chair, her skirts up.

CLOTHES WORN IN ACT II

Dracula wears his dress suit, covered by a long inverness cape, with a lining of deep purple.

Lucy wears the negligee of Act I. Van Helsing wears the same clothes of Act I. Harker has changed to either a dark blue business suit or a dark brown one, whichever doesn't conflict with the others. Renfield, in this Act as in all Acts, should be dressed in a knockabout dark gray suit. He is a bit dishevelled, but should not be made to look dirty or too unkempt. Renfield should not play the part exaggeratedly emotional. There are moments when he is extremely lucid. He has been a gentleman, of course. When he is the lunatic there are times when he has great sympathetic appeal, almost childlike in its quality. He is in awe and fear of Dracula, but at no time should his terror assume the proportions of *wild* shrieks or squeals. He makes his stage crossings with little short steps or runs, and he may play, with his head sort of crouched into his neck. One extremely important note in regard to Renfield is that he must *not* be handled brutally by the Attendant.

The choking scene offstage L., close to the end of the Second Act, is done by Renfield, the Maid and the Attendant. After the Maid screams three times, in as bloodcurdling a voice as she possibly can produce the effect, she rushes through the stage entrance to the audience of the theatre, and finds a place in the back of the auditorium and sits in the last row. At the cue of Dracula about to bite Lucy in the neck, Maid lets forth a half-scream, half-moan, and leaves the theatre before the lights come up at the Curtain. The scream in the audience at the end of Act Two is extremely important, because it relieves the emotions of the audience just as the Curtain comes down. This scream will cause a laugh, which is just what is necessary to relieve these pent-up emotions of the people.

As to the playing of the people in this Act, Dracula, of course, is played suavely and at times a bit sinister, especially in his scene with Van Helsing. When he makes his entrance through the arch upstage L., near the end of Act II, he stands holding the cape covering his eyes as the green spot comes on. Then he lowers it as he goes to position down R.

Renfield plays his scenes in this Act as in all Acts, at times half sane and the other times as the lunatic. There should be a distinct note of pathos from the point in the Act when he says to Lucy, "You are so young, so beautiful——" and at his exit is nearly sobbing as he is being led off.

Lucy, through this Act, is in a semi-hypnotized condition.

Van Helsing plays this Act, as well as all Acts, with a tremendous sincerity of purpose.

Seward, in this Act, now believes there are such things as vampires, and he is giving every assistance to Van Helsing.

Attendant, of course, plays his opening scene for laughs, and there are a great number of laughs in this scene.

Maid will get many laughs if she doesn't play it *obviously* for laughs. The high point of her scene with Attendant is her fright when he shows her the mouse, her running across stage and clambering on the chair, standing there shivering and crying in her fright.

At the end of the Act, after the scream of the

lunatic and the girl offstage L., she enters perfectly naturally, going into a semi-trance on the line that is marked in the script, "Here, Miss Lucy——" as she hands Lucy the smelling salts. From then on she walks as though in a dream.

Dracula, in this Act, wears his inverness cape.

Van Helsing wears the same clothes as in Act I.

Harker has now changed to a lounging suit of any color, so long as it doesn't conflict with Dr. Seward's suit, which also should be a lounging or business suit.

Maid wears the same clothes as in Act I.

Lucy wears the same negligee as in Act I.

Attendant uses the same uniform. Would suggest that he not wear a white coat in any of his Scenes in the play.

Renfield wears the same clothes all through the show.

ACT III

The trick chair used in this Act is extremely effective when used just after the opening, and as Van Helsing and Dr. Seward are onstage, the Doctor with his head on his hand at the R. Upper end of the desk, the Professor pacing up and down-stage up R. Neither the Professor nor Dr. Seward should be looking at this chair when it moves. This stunt is to give the idea that Dracula has come in the window upstage L., the chair, which has been turned toward the window at rise of curtain slowly turns in toward desk, as though Dracula were seating himself, and the chair takes position as though Dracula had sat down and was about to listen to the two men. At cue the chair turns out again, as though Dracula had heard all he wished to know, and about a second after it stops turning the curtains flap out.

When Renfield makes his entrance in this Act, the audience will give vent to a terrific scream if he first thrusts his hand through the door as he opens it a crack, and lets it move down slowly as though about to take hold of the knob (his body still is not seen), and as Dr. Seward speaks the line, "What fresh horrors——" etc., for Renfield to violently kick the door as he almost tumbles into the room.

When Renfield is choked by Dracula, the effect is highly intensified if Renfield staggers back toward the divan, half-gasping, half-choking, and falls at the edge of the ground cloth, in front of the divan, picking out his spot so that Dracula, when he is trapped by the three men, may have the space to walk between Renfield and the divan in order to make the circling sweep around down-stage in front of the divan and maneuvering into his position up back of the divan for his long speech to Van Helsing, Harker and Dr. Seward.

In regard to the disappearance of Dracula before the eyes of the audience and without dimming the lights, use a special star (or elevator) trap. This particular piece of business calls for a special (inverness) cape, long enough to cover Dracula's heels, with a special metal (aluminum or copper) framework for the hood. This framework fits over the shoulders and has a movable part that is sewed to the hood which Dracula throws over his head at the cue, "God's daybreak——"

While this is a tremendously effective trick, it isn't absolutely necessary to the success of the play if the producer doesn't wish to go to the expense of the trap and the cape or in the event that it would be impossible to put a trap underneath the stage and let Dracula make his escape through the left-hand side of the bookcase.

If the trap *is* used, Dracula, of course, turns upstage when Dr. Seward says, "The clouds are coloring——" etc., and, when turning, throws the hood over his head. He takes his position on the trap and Harker and Dr. Seward are ordered by Van Helsing, "Be ready when he collapses——" at which cue Dr. Seward rushes to the stage R. shoulder of Dracula and Harker to the stage L. shoulder, and both hold the metal framework upright, so that after Dracula has been lowered through the trap and the trap closed by the special plate covered with carpet, it still appears to the audience that Dracula is in the cape that the two men are holding. When Dracula is out of sight and the trap sprung, Harker and the Doctor struggle across and down L. stage as though still holding Dracula inside the cloak, and as they get near the desk they drop it to the floor to show the audience there is nothing inside. There are several spots in the next speech, where Harker and the Professor step on the middle of the cloak (being careful not to step on the small metal frame which has been on Dracula's shoulders), to show that there is nothing in it.

If this trick is used, I would suggest that the minute the audience is able to see there is nothing in the cloak, to have the flash at the fireplace *immediately*, because if you wait for the applause on this trick (and the applause is bound to come if the wait is too long) it stops the play. The audience begins to buzz, asking each other how the trick is done.

The stake and hammer on the table which are used with the trap business (if the trap is used) is what is called in magic "mis-direction." To explain: Dracula's cape, of course, describes a semicircle as it hangs on his shoulders and covers him to his feet. When the trap starts down, the corners of the trap hole show plainly to the audience in the gallery and balcony, so we have put in the piece of mis-direction by having Harker say, "Quick, Professor, the stake——" As the Professor goes to the table to pick up the stake and the hammer, the eyes of the audience follow him, and by the time he has picked up the stake Dracula has been lowered out of sight, the trap plate is back in place and the business goes on as in the script. In order to trick the audience further, when the trap is used, have a rug laid on the bias across the top of the trap, a square hole being cut in the center of the carpet, or rug, that should be woven with many small figures. Of course, the carpet on the top of the elevator must be exactly the same as the piece of carpet that is on the top of the plate which is slid in and locked after the trap is down.

When Van Helsing brings Renfield into the room to be used as bait so that the Professor can return and find Dracula attempting to kill Renfield—at the part where Professor presses the button, all the lights blackout except the fireplace, which should shine directly on Dracula's face when he enters through the window. stealing in with blue foots, making just a barely discernible blue atmosphere in the room, in order that the audience can see Renfield when he crawls on his stomach over to Dracula for the choking scene.

When Dracula endeavors to escape, after being caught by Van Helsing, about to choke Renfield, he first endeavors to get through Van Helsing to the double doors. The Host in Van Helsing's hand prevents this. Then Dracula, in order to play a little trick of his own, starts as though about to make his escape by quickly rushing toward the door down L., but at the proper point he swerves and rushes toward the arch up L., where Harker enters with the crucifix in his hand and prevents him. At about the same time Harker enters the room, Dr. Seward should enter also, through the door down L.

Timed perfectly, this piece of business will not get a laugh, but if Dracula makes three attempts to escape from the room (viz.: through Van Helsing, through Harker, through Dr. Seward), this will bring a laugh which is not good at this point.

In Attendant's scene with Dr. Seward and Van Helsing, I have found that if he speaks his exit line, "I am no *mounting* goat——" it will get a much greater laugh than if he uses the correct English—mountain goat.

In this Act Renfield makes his escape through the R. side of the bookcase. He should at no time tip off the fact that there is this means of escape by going directly to the bookcase. Rather he should stand a little bit to the side, as though he knows there must be some way out of the room but is not sure just where this exit is located.

In Lucy's scenes all through this Act, and especially her scene with Harker, the actress playing this role should endeavor to project a dual personality or a Dr. Jekyll and Mr. Hyde effect all through these lines. Her first line, on the couch, "Dawn, I hate the dawn," is a Mr. Hyde, or in this play the vampire, showing through. "How can people like daylight——" is read in a different tone and a different inflection and shows a bit of the Dr. Jekyll, or in the case of this play the real Lucy Seward, and so on all through this scene. A very effective piece of business on Lucy's part, is where Harker is brokenhearted at the change in Lucy and, as marked in the script, he puts his head in her lap. At this point she raises her arms, with elbows bent and fingers like talons, as though she were a bat about to swoop down and tear him to pieces. Just as she reaches a point where her bent elbows are on a level with her shoulders, Harker gives a little sob, which brings back the real Lucy for a second and she is all sympathy.

The clothes worn in this Act by Dracula are the same as he wore in the Second Act, *i.e.*, dress suit and a long cape. He can use the same cloak as in Act II, unless the trap is used, which calls for a special cloak containing a framework. This framework should not be over twelve inches long when the hood metal is folded so that the hood falls back on Dracula s back.

The same clothes are worn by the other members of the cast, with the exception of Lucy. She looks much better in an evening or dinner dress of some dark material, preferably green.

At the blackout after Renfield's escape, the change should be made as quickly as possible, in order that the audience will not lose the thread of the story. I have found it effective to have somebody hammering all through the change, or at least a part of the change.

ACT III (SCENE II)

This scene is much more effective if played through a dark or navy blue gauze drop. When the Curtain goes up it is absolutely black on the stage, all lights in the theatre backstage should be turned out if the black cyclorama is used instead of the booked flats, because light is liable to shine through the black cloth of the cyclorama. When Harker comes on the stage, after the entrance of Van Helsing and Dr. Seward, he should shield this light (lantern) with his hand while offstage, because this light might shine through the black cyclorama also.

While it is effective to use two 1000 watt spots hanging on the balcony ledge, controlled by the switchboard, and irised down to just the necessary light (blue medium) to be thrown on the gauze drop if it is used, they can be dispensed with. Be sure there is no spill from these lamps if used. The green spot on the coffin does not come up until the cue, marked in the script.

The dummy of Dracula, which should be life-size, is placed in the coffin so that when the front leaf is let down about one-half of the dummy can be seen. The dummy is on its back with the face looking up toward the ceiling. When the Professor and Dr. Seward endeavor to lift up the top lid of the coffin they should give the idea that it is tremendously heavy. This coffin should be painted with some deep blue medium or else resemble discolored stone. A piece of sashcord should be nailed from the side of the coffin to the lid in order that the latter will not swing back too far. Dr. Seward can speak whatever lines necessary back of the coffin lid without any difficulty, even though this lid is up. An effective piece of business is to use two small flashlight bulbs with a blue medium, controlled by the switch on the batteries, lying at the side of Dracula's head, which can be turned on by Van Helsing and turned off again when necessary when Van Helsing speaks the line, "See his face. He is crumbling away——" This entire scene must be played in a very dim light, or the whole effect will be lost.

When the stake is driven through Dracula's heart, the thud will be much more effective if the box is mixed with sand and sawdust. As he has groaned his last, Renfield rises to his full height and becomes a sane person, showing in the dim light the release from the power of the vampire. Lucy, too, when she makes her entrance, just after they kill Dracula with the stake, shows that she has been released from the evil power also.

At the end of this scene the house Curtain drops, and if the gauze is used the gauze is taken up back of the house Curtain and the divided black drop let in so that when the Curtain rises again, after the white foots have been thrown up (the house lights, however, have not as yet been thrown on) the actors may slide through the slit in this black curtain to take their positions for their bows without the audience viewing the scenery. If the audience is allowed to see the coffin and the black cyclorama and the rest of the paraphernalia backstage in this last Scene of the play it is bound to kill the thrill they have had and mitigate the success of putting over the Curtain speech. This latter point, by the way, is one of the best parts of the play.

Almost immediately the Curtain has risen, after the end of the play, Van Helsing steps forward a step or two, holds up his hand to quiet the applause of the audience who are about to file out, and makes his speech. He practically kids them all through until he reaches the words, "There are such things——" This is read melodramatically, which throws the chill back into their marrows and sends them out of the theatre quaking.

"DRACULA"

PUBLICITY THROUGH YOUR LOCAL PAPERS

The press can be an immense help in giving publicity to your productions. In the belief that the best reviews from the New York and other large papers are always interesting to local audiences, and in order to assist you, we are printing below several excerpts from those reviews.

To these we have also added a number of suggested press notes which may be used either as they stand or changed to suit your own ideas and submitted to the local press.

"——treating of this weird farce as a mystery, they send the customary shivers of apprehension streaming down the back and 'Dracula' holds the audience nervously expectant."—"*New York Times.*"

"'Dracula,' which somebody will have to club to death if it's ever to stop, is still profitably a-tour— It will presently play Brooklyn for the fourth or fifth time."—"*New York Sunday Times.*"

"An evening rich in horror."—"*New York Telegram.*"

"Nothing more blithely blood-curdling since 'The Bat.' "—"*New York Herald-Tribune.*"

"See it and creep."—"*New York Evening Post.*"

"Was enjoyed to the hilt—audience quaked delightedly."—"*New York World.*"

"Should be seen by all who love their marrows jolted."—"*New York Sun.*"

"Dracula" has been described by critics as a play for people that like their coffee strong. There is no mistake about this thriller being of the type that will shock the staunchest of playgoers who like thrilling plays—it deals with the supernatural and there is no awkward explanation at its conclusion. Playgoers who visit the —————— Theatre next week to witness the performance of the —————— Players will go away with the satisfaction of having had more thrills than ever before in their lives inside of a theatre, for the great vampire play, "Dracula," is a real thriller that, speaking literally, has raised hair on millions of scalps since the date of its original production in England several years ago, where it has been playing ever since, to say nothing of the long run it has enjoyed in the United States.

The patrons of the popular —————— Players at the —————— Theatre will have an ample feast of the mysterious, uncanny and the supernatural all next week, for the great vampire play of "Dracula" is listed for production at that time. This thriller is a dramatization of Bram Stoker's novel of the same name, originally published in England many years ago, and a novel that ever since has had a most phenomenal sale all over the English-speaking world.

Mystery plays have been produced before now at the popular —————— Theatre, and on previous occasions patrons of the —————— Players have been thrilled and chilled, but "Dracula," the next offering of the popular players, is so remarkable in its thrills and so completely overwhelming in every respect that it is bound to prove a rare treat of the season. Local theatregoers are warned in advance

that it would be wise for them to visit a specialist
and have their hearts examined before subjecting
them to the fearful thrills and shocks that "Dracula"
holds in store for them.

Theatre-goers who enjoy a quick-fire procession
of super-quality thrills, surprises, shudders and sen-
sations cannot afford to miss seeing "Dracula," the
mystery of mysteries, that Manager —————— of
the —————— Theatre has selected as the next attraction for the —————— Players beginning next
Monday evening. For years "Dracula" has been
thrilling England and is still playing to capacity audiences. It was the outstanding hit of the season at
the Fulton Theatre, New York, and has since been
touring the country, from Maine to California. It is
said that audiences everywhere have found the two
hours of horror, surprises and thrills that invariably
greet this play wherever played to be not only blood-
curdling but most entertaining as well. "Dracula"
even caused the most hardened of the "Now show
me's" to shudder and shiver in their seats, and advance reports promise that it will be the jolliest kind
of blood-curdler imaginable.

The play was founded on Bram Stoker's famous
novel of the same name, which has been read by
two generations of booklovers, and though it is more
than thirty years since it was first published, it has
run through countless editions and still ranks as
one of the best sellers.

Local theatregoers will get a real thrill next week
at the —————— Theatre when the ——————
Players will present that thrilling, chilling mystery
vampire play, "Dracula." Other thrillers are said to
be bedtime stories compared to this narrative of
the supernatural.

SYNOPSIS

Lucy Seward, daughter of the physician in charge of a sanatorium near London, is mysteriously anæmic. Doctor Van Helsing, a specialist in obscure diseases, suspects a vampire which, according to legend, is an ugly soul that, grave-bound by day, roams the earth at night, and sustains its earthly life by sucking the blood of approachable victims. Instituting a search, Van Helsing uncovers Count Dracula as such a vampire and, finding the grave, drives a stake through the heart of the corpse from which he comes, thus ending the vampire's existence.

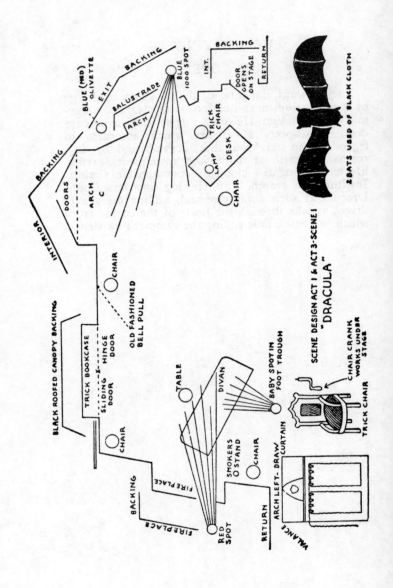

SCENE DESIGN ACT I & ACT 3-SCENE I
"DRACULA"

2 BATS USED OF BLACK CLOTH

CHAIR CRANK WORKS UNDER STAGE

TRICK CHAIR

BLACK ROOFED CANOPY BACKING

TRICK BOOKCASE

SLIDING HINGE DOOR

OLD FASHIONED BELL PULL

INTERIOR

BACKING

DOORS

ARCH C

ARCH

ARCH

BALUSTRADE

BACKING

EXIT

BLUE (MED) OLIVETTE

BLUE 1000 SPOT

BACKING

INT.

DOOR OPENS ON STAGE

RETURN

TRICK CHAIR

LAMP

DESK

CHAIR

CHAIR

CHAIR

TABLE

DIVAN

BABY SPOT IN FOOT TROUGH

SMOKERS STAND

CHAIR

FIREPLACE

FIREPLACE

BACKING

RED SPOT

RETURN

ARCH LEFT-DRAW CURTAIN

VALANCE

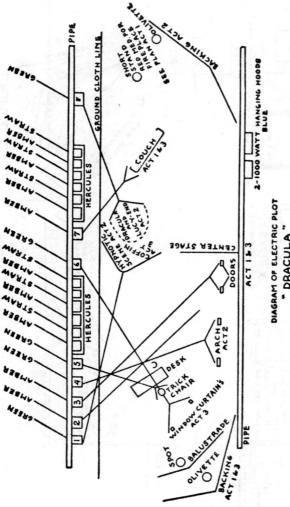

DIAGRAM OF ELECTRIC PLOT
"DRACULA"

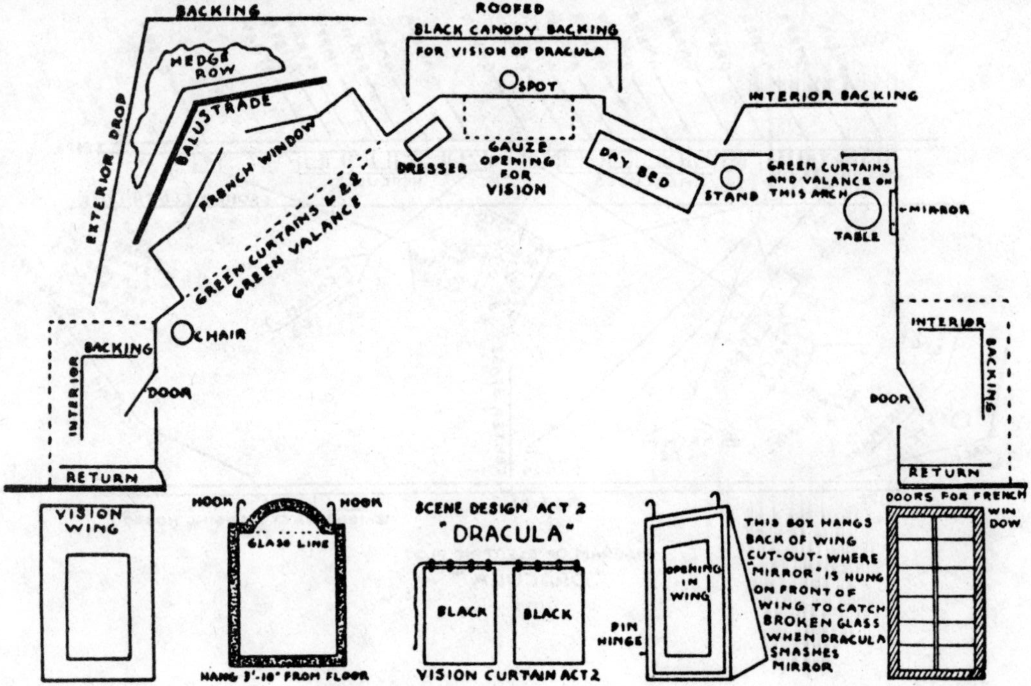
BACKING
HEDGE ROW
BALUSTRADE
EXTERIOR DROP
FRENCH WINDOW
GREEN CURTAINS & ££
GREEN VALANCE
ROOFED
BLACK CANOPY BACKING
FOR VISION OF DRACULA
SPOT
DRESSER
GAUZE OPENING FOR VISION
DAY BED
STAND
INTERIOR BACKING
GREEN CURTAINS AND VALANCE ON THIS ARCH
MIRROR
TABLE
CHAIR
BACKING
INTERIOR
DOOR
RETURN
INTERIOR
BACKING
DOOR
RETURN
VISION WING
HOOK
HOOK
GLASS LINE
HANG 3'-10" FROM FLOOR
SCENE DESIGN ACT 2
"DRACULA"
BLACK
BLACK
VISION CURTAIN ACT 2
OPENING IN WING
PIN HINGE
THIS BOX HANGS BACK OF WING CUT-OUT- WHERE "MIRROR" IS HUNG ON FRONT OF WING TO CATCH BROKEN GLASS WHEN DRACULA SMASHES MIRROR
DOORS FOR FRENCH WIN DOW